LEILA SEGAL

BREATHE
Stories from Cuba

lubin & kleyner
london

Breathe - Stories from Cuba

This book is typeset in Trebuchet MS and
Palatino from Linotype GmbH

lubin & kleyner, london
an imprint of flipped eye publishing
www.flippedeye.net

ISBN: 978-0-9541570-5-0

LOTTERY FUNDED

Supported using public funding by
ARTS COUNCIL
ENGLAND

To my mother and father

BREATHE

LEILA SEGAL

Acknowledgements

I am deeply grateful to my editor, Nii Ayikwei Parkes, for his skill and care, and for his belief in this book, and to my publisher, flipped eye, for its commitment to its writers. I would like to thank Karen McCarthy Woolf, Niki Aguirre, Dinorah Del Aguila Garcia, Linda Leatherbarrow, Pippa Hockton, Jacqueline Crooks and Nathalie Teitler for their encouragement and support. Thanks to The Arts Council England for its generous assistance, and to Charles Beckett for his advice. My profound appreciation and gratitude go to my family, and friends in Cuba and the UK, without whose love I could not walk this road.

Contents

GLOSSARY

SIEMPRE LUCHANDO

I WENT OUT for the night with Ángel although I hardly knew him yet.

We caught a shell of a car from Calle 23 down towards the Capitolio to meet his French friends, 10 pesos the ride. Ángel sat in front and I crouched in the back next to a filthy rag and a plastic bottle of gasoline. The door was held together with string; its innards spilled over where the panel had fallen off. To get out you had to remove part of a wooden plank that wedged the catch shut.

The driver sounded the horn by touching a metal coil to bare wire at the centre of the wheel.

I was on the edge again, but further out than last time. We were speeding round the racetrack of Centro Habana with no lights, bitten by the night.

Dark castles sprung through the windows, catching only the white or gold of Ángel's teeth or eyes. Here and there was a family on a stoop, or a glowing yellow room.

A secret city—*desconocida*—uncharted and unknown.

We spun into the Malecón, disgorged from the car towards the group. Lady's squeaky voice angled out above the crowd; she wheeled and turned sideways, laughing with her friend.

The French boy perched next to them on the Malecón wall, kicking his feet against the side. They were drinking rum from plastic cups, with a bottle of tuKola bought from the store. Ángel spoke to them in evening-class French, while I gazed out over the sea. Beyond the rocks a small boat was fishing and another country bore down from 90 miles of ocean grave.

Some time later we walked to the Barrio Chino for our meal.

The restaurant table was still wet: it was so humid that nothing would dry from the rain. Ángel and I sat together at one end. He leaned in urgently, his voice low so that the others wouldn't hear. He wanted to talk about Sabine.

"Me da pena contigo," he said—*I have let you down*. He seemed unable to halt the flow from head to mouth, and used his whole body to explain. "I *sorry*, Louise. Last week when we went out, you did not know the situation. Sabine—she called to me and said: I have to see you, I miss you.

"So I thought, if Louise comes too, it will draw less attention. And then we had a kind of discusión—how you say?—a fight. We went to buy the rum and cola—do you remember? Her novio, Marc, he told for us to go. For her to go and me to accompany her. It was a time when we could talk and embrace, and Sabine she said to me: Who is the English woman? Why are you dancing with *her*?"

I could hardly believe that Sabine was jealous of me. Then I remembered her cold stare when we were introduced, how she'd blanked me when I said we were neighbours. Sabine's boyfriend Marc had come to visit from Paris, but he didn't know Sabine was sleeping with Ángel. She spent her time tormenting Ángel, inviting him to join her and Marc, calling at all hours, even though Ángel rose at five to reach his office in Miramar, saying that she needed him. At first he refused, but when he finally gave in and went to see her, Sabine made love to Marc right under Ángel's nose.

Ángel touched my hand. "I tell Sabine I can not see her while he is here. But her novio he wanted to do a little—you know—*business*." He held up his forefinger and thumb and rubbed them together. "So I thought, just for to do the business—he wanted to buy some cigars. And it turned out somehow that we were all sitting together in a concert—Sabine, her novio and me—and she kept turning to look at me, staring into my eyes.

"At first I looked back—to give her something, you know? But then I got up and left, and afterwards I told her: I can not be together with you in that place. Sabine, what you are doing is wrong."

Prostitutes strolled in twos and threes up and down Calle Cuchillo. One wore an outfit of silver Lycra—bell-bottoms and a boob-tube that was too small. She seemed to boil over the top of her clothes, her belly flopping forwards above the waistband of her trousers.

We sat waiting for the food, attended by Asian Cubans who wore judo shirts tied at the waist over black flares. Lady and her friend were squeezed onto the bench opposite me, while I sat hip-to-thigh with the French boy.

"*Joder* is the word for fuck in Spanish," he was saying.

"No, no, no," said Lady.

"Sí, es Joder."

Lady exchanged looks with her friend from under the eyelashes but said nothing.

"*Singar*," I said. "Singar is the word for fuck in Cuba."

"Who taught you that?" asked Lady.

"My husband."

"You have a husband here in Cuba?"

"Yes."

"Where is he?"

"In Pinar del Río, working."

Snorts of laughter from the French boy. "You know what the Cubans say about the Pinareños?" he said. "They make jokes about them the way you do about the Irish."

The girls were listening, somewhere on the verge of hysterical laughter, their eyes wide open, mouths hanging slack.

"They built a cinema in Pinar del Río," he continued, beads of sweat on his upper lip, "and when they finished, the workmen couldn't find the crane. You know where it was?"

His crooked eyes were without colour and strange folds of double chin hung around his neck.

"They had left it inside the building!"

Shrieks of laughter from the girls.

"What does your husband do?" asked Lady.

"Does he build cinemas?" said the French boy, almost beside himself.

"No he—"

"Mira cómo le da pena!" said Lady delightedly.

"—he works in tourism."

"And do you see him from time to time?" the French boy panned around the table. "When his Cuban wife's away?"

Lady's friend stretched her mouth into a grin, but one eye—the right one—closed itself to me in a wink.

Just before midnight we drove to Club Cóctel—*Ángel, take us somewhere real,* the French boy said, *not some tourist shit*—where we joined the crowd waiting on La Rampa to be let in.

A man in a string vest stood on the corner, curled around his woman, stroking her face. The woman wore bright pink lipstick and looked up at me, narrowing her crow's-feet eyes.

Ángel put his palm out, begging for a dollar, so sly I hardly knew he'd done it. His engineer's salary didn't stretch to nights out with foreign friends. He scuffed his feet and dragged his head as I peeled off the bill and handed it to him.

Inside we danced, packed into a tiny dark room. At first, all I could make out was a curl of gold, a dread, and white teeth on black. Whites of eyes on pitch faces made Ángel's mulatto seem light and he, somehow, not to belong. Sweat ran off my face, in a river under my dress, and down between the blades of my back. Sometimes I was crushed against other bodies, but never pushed. Clean faces, nice clothes, no trouble.

I could look because it wasn't looking, it was listening, and we were all listening together—dancing, conducting symphonies, rapt.

The Cubans sang in a language they didn't understand, straight from the West Coast—raised their arms, did the hip hop salute, jumped and jacked to the beat. And from above a corner of the bar, *The Box* delivered a non-stop stream of rappers and babes from the USA.

Big jails to hide niggas, their mouths shaped, hands raised in praise; *niggas scratching for bread,* they mimed with 8Ball, dreaming in time. For a second I was looking down, as if on a bridge watching two trains about to collide, understanding alone; then a man was asking over and over if I would dance, and Ángel was standing next to me, his arm around my waist.

"Where you from?" the man said to Ángel.

"Soy cubano."

"Sorry, brother. Te oí hablando inglés." He held out his hand.

Ángel took my elbow and steered me round the crowd. We danced together for some time, but only once did he look me in the eye. He was lost in thought—of Sabine, perhaps, lying somewhere with her novio.

A man who looked like Tupac danced next to us, while his girlfriend peered through glasses and tightly braided hair. We smiled. Her hips were swinging slightly, and so were mine.

She came to stand in front of me. Her dress had red, pink and white flowers on it, and a frill along the edge. Her hips moved, her belly moved, she cupped a hand in front to measure the beat. As she caught me in her time, her eyes leaped and laughed to mirror mine.

She told me something I didn't hear, so I leaned in.

"You are like my sister," she said.

The French boy, dancing nearby, threw me a lopsided smile. His canvas shoulder-bag was slung diagonally across billowing folds of white cotton on his chest. He jogged up and down, slicing his arms like scissors by his waist, and slapped his feet down duck-like to the beat.

Lady sat bedraggled on a bar stool with her friend, holding off the crowd, which squeezed itself into every corner of the room. Her eyeliner had run and she looked tired.

The French group, crushed around them, looked bored and marginally afraid. When Los Aldeanos came on, one of them, a stout girl, broke into a furious elephantine jig, snapping her fingers and knocking against those around the well of space she'd cleared. Her face was frozen, mouth and eyes turned down, her white vest stained with sweat.

I was held from both sides, swaying on my feet.

Ángel looked at me.

"Shall we go?" he said.

We turned left outside the club and walked up Calle M towards the palms of the Hotel Nacional. Ángel skulked along beside me through the polished wood and marble foyer, out to the chairs by the sea. It was very quiet, just one couple sipping tea.

I sat on the sofa. Each time I moved, it drew him to me—drew his eye and body as one piece of a puzzle fits, unknowing, to the other.

Ángel sank his thin frame into the folds of a chair, white shirt slung low over camel pants, his face a sculpture of bone and ragged jaw.

"What do you think about love?" he said.

I stared into a black patch of sky beyond the balustrade. Time had shortened or lengthened to a point, like reflecting mirrors that trap you in a single frame, and I was grasping at the past, the future, living this moment for him.

"What are your plans? What are your hopes?"—he was fidgeting now and had already finished his tea, fingers dancing along the armrest—*scratchin*—as his mouth formed the words. "In Cuba we do not have hopes and we can not not make plans. I live for today, siempre luchando—always I struggle. Every day I move, and I survive. I find a way to distract myself. I must always be outside, find a way to forget my life. I can not sit in my house, it makes me crazy."

Ángel lived with his parents. There was a place for him in the spare room but whenever guests came, or other members of the family needed the room, he had to sleep on the sofa. His seven-year-old daughter lived with her mother nearby. And until the Spring he had been in love with a Frenchwoman—Juliette. She had been his hope and his future. Sometimes Juliette would come to visit, making promises that she forgot upon her return to France.

One day, she wrote to Ángel and told him that he could come: if he found a way to get to France she would help him start a new life. So he saved for a year on a salary of $15 a month, then Juliette began a doctorate and put aside their plan.

Now, there was a new French girl, Sabine, and a new hope—as long as she wanted to fall in love.

Ángel looked up at the sky and so did I. His eyes were black hollows, inches from mine.

"Siempre luchando." He gazed out at the sea then sank back into his chair. "Yes, I hope to go to France later in the year. This time I hope to go."

SWIMMING

CAPTIVE TO THE heat, she was unable to breathe. She decided to get up and go to the salón, where Nelidah would already be preparing lessons. She would read till Javier woke. She glanced over at him. He had one arm flung forward and the other squashed beneath his ribs. His large hands looked dry. She took one and curled her palm into it, his fingers around hers like a black spider she'd seen squatting on the bathroom floor the evening before.

She was in a rocker looking at photographs on the salón wall when Javier emerged. The photographs showed Nelidah as a young woman — with long, heavy hair, square glasses and a fringe — just after the Revolution, around 1960, she said.

Javier sat down in the rocker opposite. He wore a white shirt and pressed trousers. She wanted to touch him, to hold his hand, feel his arm around her shoulders. In his presence she was seldom not touching him — it was natural, the same here for every woman with her man.

Nelidah disappeared into the kitchen. Through the serving hatch came the crackling of oil over gas, and a rancid smell, which made her suspect that this was not the first time

Nelidah had used the oil.

Already, she could hardly move in the thick, close air. The fan turned back and forth; Javier tapped his toes in time. His chancletas were white—they were hers but he'd taken to wearing them in the house.

"Breakfast," Nelidah called.

They sat at the kitchen table. She ate slices of mango from a small, chipped dish. Nelidah put plates in front of each of them, with well-fried eggs and dry white bread. The meal wasn't included—it cost a dollar each, added to the bill for the room. She left the eggs but Javier ate his and asked for more.

"What do you want to do today?" he said, pushing away the plate.

"To be in the water."

"She wants to be in the water. She's like a fish!" said Nelidah in a high voice. "Take her to the Playa beach."

She did not want to go to the beach. There were no sunshades and they would have to huddle under her black umbrella on the baking sand.

"Let's go to the pool," she said. "At the hotel."

"Maybe. But for sure not if you wear that"—he tugged at her loose, faded smock—"You'll have to change. Vete. Cámbiate—before it gets too hot."

She went to the stairs, but instead of going up to the room, paused at their foot and turned to look back at Javier and Nelidah, whom she could see framed in the light of the kitchen door. Javier was sitting on his chair and Nelidah on another, facing him. He had grown a moustache since her last visit and the old woman was reaching out to touch his face.

"You haven't changed your ideas?" Nelidah was saying.

He pulled away. "I arranged a car—"

"—and Marisol?"

"Marisol will wait." He leaned back in his chair. "Ella entiende."

"I'm afraid in my heart for you," said Nelidah.

"But I have to keep her close."

"The block is talking. What do I tell them?" Nelidah touched the gold locket at her throat and rose from the chair, picking up the greasy plates.

Javier stood and went to the fridge. He took out a beer and closed the fridge with hardly a sound, even though it was an old and heavy door.

The white-tiled stairs were cold under her bare feet. Dust caught in her throat. She clawed at her neck, then swept off the old smock and threw it onto the bed. She put on her best blue shirt-dress, leaving the bottom two buttons open. The voices in the kitchen continued. She must go back—they should not be allowed to go on without her.

"Guapa!" said Nelidah when she returned to the table. "Más gordita!"

"I'm not fat."

"It is beautiful. Fatter is good," said Nelidah.

"The last two buttons must be closed," said Javier.

"He's jealous. You have a tattoo on your thigh!" said Nelidah and winked. The skin on her breast where the locket lay was burnt and crepey from the sun.

She closed the buttons and reached for Javier's hand. Javier accepted her hand and held it as he raised a tiny coffee cup to his lips with his other hand. "You don't look very good," he said, draining the last few drops. "You should eat." She glanced up at Nelidah, who was dusting a row of plastic ornaments with care, and tried to catch her eye. "Ah, you two," said Nelidah turning away. "The lovers." She thought that Nelidah must be smiling, but the muscles in the back of the old woman's neck tightened and she said, "Leave me the money for last night on the table before you go."

They walked down Calle 2 through warm spits of rain. She took photographs of crumbling, broken things and tripped over potholes. Through the light, the rain was acid, burning cold on heat, and perfect fuchsia hearts flowered in foliage that overtook the street.

They came to Burgui. The restaurant took up one side of a rubbish-strewn parking lot, set back from the street. An old man worked the tables, pulling and pushing chairs, creating an unnecessary sweat. He wore a stained, dirty-smart sun-shirt pulled over beige trousers. In her country she would have guessed he was homeless, working for pennies, but here it was hard to tell. A girl—15 maybe—stood with a cloth beside the bar.

"Sit," Javier said, pulling out a white plastic chair. "We must wait for my cousin. You ate nothing at breakfast—what will you have?"

"I don't want anything." She was hungry but did not want to eat on the street—you could catch an infection called giardia, which lodged itself inside your digestive tract and consumed your internal organs one by one.

"Make us a bifstek, hermano," Javier told the cook.

She tried to look comfortable and relaxed, then realised that the serving man had stopped wiping tables and was just standing there staring at her.

"And give me a Bucanero," Javier called to the girl at the bar.

"Sí," the girl said with a blank stare.

The meat came greasy, squelching in oil in a red paper bag, and the chips were more fat than potato, but Javier pushed it over and she ate it anyway. "Is it nice?" he asked. She nodded, her mouth full.

Across the parking lot, by a row of bins, a very small black girl in a pink towelling boob-tube and shorts hugged her mother's thigh. The mother squatted astride a chair, smoking, a white turban on her head. She lifted one finger off the back of the chair at Javier, who caught her eye. The child laughed and ran to him.

"Qué quieres?" he said, pushing her away.

Fat from the grill rose in the air; she tried not to breathe too deeply. Javier curled his fingers around the dark brown bottle-neck and took a swig. He seemed angry but she couldn't be sure. His eyes were narrow and slanted. She remembered that the Chinese had come to Cuba long ago and bred in.

"Do you like it here?" he asked.

"When will we go to the pool?" She was not able to decide who the woman in the white turban was and whether Javier knew her.

After two beers it began to rain again.

"My cousin will not come today," Javier said. He stood up. "Let's go."

The bill was 20 pesos. She pushed a note to Javier across the table and he paid at the bar.

As they walked to the street they were followed by the tiny whining girl. "Qué quieres?" Javier said, turning sharply. There was a look of deep disgust on his face. The child's boob-tube had slipped down and bunched up over her bloated belly. She covered her face with her hands. "Vete! Ahora, ve a tu mamá!" said Javier.

He turned his back and they continued on the way.

"Where is your bag?" Javier asked, after they had been walking for a few minutes. "You have left it at the restaurant."

This was true. "I must go back," she said, and began to run, but the pavement was crowded and no one seemed to notice that she was trying to get through. She pushed forward then realised Javier was not with her, and stopped. He was several yards behind, walking at his usual pace.

"Con calma," he said as he reached her. "Everything is achieved with calm."

"But my bag! With all my things!"

"Tsk. You should be careful," said Javier. "This is Havana, you know."

At Burgui they were waiting. "We are good here. We find a bag, we put it there," said the old chair-mover pointing to the bar. He, the girl and the cook stood staring at her, lined up like skittles placed at different heights.

At Paseo herds of gangrenous cars bore down both ways. Crumbling half-inhabited grandeur petered out to buildings so dusty and broken that no one lived in them at all. Right at the bottom of the street, some prefab boxes with flapping washing met another highway. They rounded past a Benetton with windows so dark you couldn't see in, and reached the hotel's sliding doors. Two sets, separated by an airlock. She caught sight of herself in one—the blue dress had ridden up. She tugged it over her knees.

Javier took off his sunglasses, wiped them, and pulled them back on.

"Ready?" He took her hand and guided her before him into the lobby.

The hotel was all marble, lush and quiet, patrolled by uniformed guards. They took a smooth glide up the escalator and more doors slid open onto a cut-glass blue pool where pale bodies exhausted from their lives fried, and European women in expensive clothes smoked and looked at fashion magazines.

They walked over to the booth where the man in fake Ray-Bans asks for your guest number then issues towels and a mat.

Javier gave her an almost imperceptible nod.

Five dollars, folded in three. She put it on the counter. The man looked at it and her.

"Wait." He motioned with his head to a colleague inside

the booth. Javier's face was reflected next to hers in the man's sunglasses—Javier looked like an impostor: a black Cuban with a guest. It went against all her instincts to wait—she wanted to leave now, not stand here and be caught.

The colleague came out, looked slowly at the bill and said, "No. Today the boss is here. Another time."

They slipped away, down the stairs and across the acres of marble lobby. Javier had a scowl on his face.

"Let's go for a walk along the Malecón," she said to change the mood, but before he could answer she started to cough.

"I need a glass of water," she said to Javier.

"You won't get one here."

Through a large window, the sea pounded the Malecón sending up ribbons of foam, but from inside it was silent, like TV with the sound turned down. She remembered a time when her mother had held her, looking down an open flight of steps. She was clutching a china shell in her hand. Her mother had told her to put it down, but she refused. "You'll drop it and it will break," her mother said. As she clung there in her mother's arms, something inside took hold and made her open her fist. The ornament fell and smashed to pieces on the steps.

TAXI

It was already 8am. Alejandro sailed through Centro Habana towards Vedado, scanning the pavements for stragglers late for work, who might be hoping to jump into a peso cab and make it on time. The sun jabbed at his sleeve and mocked the faded cloth that he had tacked up to hide the innards of the car roof.

No one. There wouldn't be a fare until at least 10 o'clock now. He stopped at Roseny's stall on the corner of J for a bun and glass of squash, then drove around Vedado for a while. Empty streets. But then he saw a fair-haired man in a smart check shirt and grey slacks, briefcase in one hand, the other held out high to hail him. A foreigner, but not a tourist—dressed for business rather than the sun.

"La Rampa?" said the man.

"Sí señor."

"Excellent," the man said, more to himself than Alejandro, and got in.

The Buick was nearly 50 years old. It had wide, bouncy leather seats, which held four at the back and three in front. Alejandro had sold his mother's jewellery to buy it, and he didn't feel good about this. Throughout the Special Period in the '90s, when people were killing cats to eat, she had kept the jewellery safe. Some things could not be sold—no matter how hard the Yankees tried to starve them into submission. But after she died, his resolve slipped away. To make himself feel better, he liked to think that the car had once belonged to a Yankee playboy, half-drunk on Cuban rum, a mulatta at his side. And then he liked to think of how, when the Revolution came, the bastard lost the Buick—the bullets, the fear, the girl running free.

"Stop here." The fair-haired man tapped him on the shoulder.

Alejandro pulled over to the kerb and the man got out, handing him a 10-peso note. Alejandro reached under the dashboard for his money bag. It was just bigger than his palm—green cloth, with a large purple flower appliquéd onto the front. He hadn't the heart to get rid of it, even though Juana had made it for him and thinking of her caused him pain. Her white cotton stitches were visible—long, baggy stitches. She'd never really learned to sew.

He had woken one morning to see her sitting on the edge of their bed stitching the green cloth, a cafecito ready for him on the desk, where his files lay open from study the night before. This was before driving the cab had taken over—he was still studying then, morning and night, sometimes rising stiff with sleep from his desk at dawn to see Juana, plump and sweet, lying across their bed.

She had *desired* him then, the promising young doctor from a good family: cultured, revolutionary, with impeccable credentials—he was the perfect complement to her intellect and ambition.

10am. He turned into Parque Central. This was always a good place to pick up fares: heat-tired people who couldn't bear to wait hours for an overcrowded bus. The taxi cost 10 pesos, wherever you wanted to go in Havana. On a good day he'd make 250 pesos—$10. Out of this he had to pay for petrol, of course, and the taxi licence, but it was still over half what he could make at the hospital in a month.

A corner group became individuals as Alejandro approached, each with an arm out waving. He came to a sudden stop, foot sharp on the brake. Three faces peered into his window.

"Eh, eh! Wait your turn!" said one, pushing to the front.

"My turn! I was here before you," said the second.

"Mira, hermano—are you going to Playa? Via Tercera?" said the third.

Alejandro had hardly said "Playa" before the door was yanked open and all three toppled forward, trying to squeeze their way in. The first, a small stocky woman, made a bridge with one arm for her husband and child to pass under, shoving the others aside.

One o'clock. The hottest hour, when any sane person would hide from the sun. Alejandro drove fast, almost missing an old woman, so fair that she could have been an albino. She was waving one arm to stop him and wore a kerchief on her head. As Alejandro drew up, she smiled and leaned into his window.

"Buenas días. Gracias señor." It was deliberately pronounced, with North American curves. Before he had a chance to speak, she tugged open the door and pulled herself in by his side.

Alejandro hesitated. He wasn't supposed to take tourists in his cab—the licence said: *Cubans and foreign residents only*. For the tourists there were modern, state-owned cars. But if today was like yesterday, with hardly a fare, it would be just frijoles again for supper. He put his foot down and drew away from the kerb.

"So, where do you want to go?" He liked to practise his English.

"To Iglesia Santa Rita—it's in Miramar—Calle 26 and Fifth."

"For a guided tour?"

"Oh goodness, no. I've come to distribute medicines. We do it through the church."

One of those. He'd met her kind before. As if their token gifts could change a thing.

His sour expression did not seem to put her off.

"I come every year at this time—to see my friends, and do what I can to help. *Me encanta Cuba.*"

Alejandro turned left into Línea. "You've been here before?"

"Sure have."

"And your home, where is that?"

"Taos, New Mexico."

He wondered why she had chosen Cuba. She didn't seem like the other American tourists, with their long-lens cameras and brand-new clothes.

"What brought you here at first?"

"It was back in the '60s. We were all young then—even your Revolución. My late husband was a pastor and we came together—drove all the way down through Mexico in our bus. My, what a journey. Churches for Change we called ourselves... his Sunday school kids painted the bus."

A warm breeze came in from the space where, had Alejandro had money to replace the glass, the car window would have been.

"Cookie?" She pulled a packet of cheap Cuban biscuits from her bag and put it on the dashboard next to his silver San Sebastián. "And you? How do you like driving a cab?"

"It's work. A man must work."

Alejandro took a biscuit; it was chocolate flavour with cream in the centre. The cream had melted into a goo that stuck to his fingers. Yes, a man must work—but at what price? Juana had been so pleased the day he bought the car. She had suggested it to him some months before as they queued at the farmer's market for plantain. Two people in front of them had argued about who was first and Juana had pulled her hand from his.

"I am sick of fighting to buy vegetables," she said. "Why can't we go to the market on 19 and B?"

"You know why," he told her. "19 and B charge double. Do you want to end up with nothing but plantain to eat?"

"I want a better life, that's what. Yusleidys' husband makes ten times what he used to since he bought his cab."

Alejandro handed Juana the sunshade he'd been holding over her head and spoke so coldly to her for the rest of the day that she did not bring the subject up again.

But he thought about it after that. Juana seemed increasingly discontented. He was finishing his internship at the hospital and working long hours; she was spending more time than ever at the university, perfecting her French and English for the final exam. Then a friend mentioned that there was a Buick going for $1,000 on his block.

It was the day Raúl Castro, brother of Fidel, had been due to visit the hospital. The administrative committee had provided new beds, sheets and towels—repainted it all. Alejandro wanted to protest that there wasn't even money to repair the out-of-service ambulance, but he kept his mouth shut of course. Then, a couple of weeks later, there was a power cut and it took a whole eight minutes for the generator to kick in. Alejandro lost a patient on a ventilator. Next day he bought the car.

"You don't like it?" The old woman tapped his forearm.

"Don't like what?"

"Your work—driving a cab?"

"Not much, but I like what it gets me."

The cab swung to one side, buffeted by a particularly strong gust of sea air.

"Gets you?"

"Yes, a better life."

"Oh, I see." She looked out of the window.

"It rests my mind. That's the best I can say for my days."

"Why should your mind need resting?"

Alejandro felt weary, incredibly weary, and had no desire to talk about his life.

The old woman shook her bag out of the window to get rid of biscuit crumbs and turned to look at him.

"Lord, your mind must be tired—it's about five minutes since I asked you that question and still no answer."

Her insistence was flattering, as if she were genuinely interested in what he had to say. He noted that she listened as he talked and took a moment to reply, which made her seem sympathetic—although, he reminded himself, nothing she had said so far actually demonstrated that fact.

"I am a medical doctor. The nights are for my tésis"—he pronounced the word the Spanish way, unsure of its English equivalent—"*A Programme for the Elimination of Dengue Fever in Cuba.*"

"Well now, I just knew that you were doing something good," she said. "A doctor—like my son, Paul. He's an oncologist at the Bellevue in New York." She frowned. "But why are you driving a cab?"

"I had to do it… A doctor's salary doesn't pay enough."

"Enough for what?" She looked at him.

"A decent life."

"You mean jeans from the dollar store and fancy food." It was under her breath, but Alejandro caught it. "Will you be going back—to medical work, I mean?" she said aloud.

"I'm not sure. I can't see how. When I've finished my

tésis—I try to continue at night—maybe then there'll be another way. Maybe things in Cuba will change." Alejandro didn't go into detail. Indiscretion was risky, even with someone who seemed harmless, like la vieja here.

He felt the wind on his face. There was more air outside the city centre; you could breathe better here. He stopped at the next set of lights and turned to look out of his side window. A group of primary school children in beetroot shorts and pinafore dresses were singing and clapping their hands.

He yawned and checked his watch. No wonder he was tired—he'd been up since 3am. This week it was his turn for guard duty outside his building. It was a communal responsibility—every adult took a turn. Fifteen years in that place. Sometimes, coming home after a day in the cab, he would take a minute to lean into the courtyard and gaze up to the top of the building. Six stories high, you could barely see the sky. The sun never shone in—only thin slivers of light landing hard on old marble floors, which tip-tapped as you walked.

The door to his room had a lock on it, but it was flimsy and break-ins were becoming more common. He pictured the room, running over possible weak spots: the table with its flowered cover and vase of dusty plastic roses, the two blue chairs, and, most importantly, his mother's dresser with its precious contents of eighty-five dollars under the paper in the bottom drawer. This was covered with Juana's blue silk kerchief, which still smelled of the Four Seasons peach conditioner that she used on her curly black hair. She'd been wearing it the night they met at the Teatro Nacional—a mutual friend had introduced them during the interval. Alejandro had become conscious that his hair was not well-combed, and began to wish that he had worn the pale blue shirt, which was cooler and didn't show perspiration marks under the arms. His skin and hair were fair, unusual in Cuba even for those of purely Spanish descent, but he had dark brown eyes and a muscular torso, which, as he asked the tall mulatta Juana whether she'd enjoyed the ballet, he drew to its full height. She replied that she had, adding that while the interpretation of Don Quixote was not a new one, it was well executed nonetheless.

The following day Alejandro called her to suggest a visit to Coppelia for ice cream. There was so much noise at her house that he had to keep asking her to repeat herself. Eventually, she'd put a hand over the mouthpiece and, in a tone quite different from the demure one that she was using with him, shouted "Shut up!" at someone in the background. Later, when Alejandro asked her whom she was shouting at, Juana said it was her father. The family shared an apartment with her aunt, uncle and cousins. Juana's father, a journalist, was out of work. He could be found most days drinking and playing dominoes on the street—which, she said, was almost a relief, because when he was in the house he would invariably start quarrels with one member of the family or another.

Alejandro and Juana had talked long after they finished their two-peso plates of coconut ice cream. That night, she returned with him to his room, where they held each other till dawn lit her face and he touched her lips with his.

Shortly afterwards, Juana left the apartment she shared with her family to move in with him.

Alejandro manoeuvred the Buick across the junction at Línea and 18, and into the tunnel that led to Miramar, the nicer part of town, where Party officials, foreigners and salsa stars lived. The houses were painted shades of pastel—peach and green and blue; outside stood trimmed gardenias, succulents and ladies' tongues in terracotta pots. Ornamental wrought iron gates shut them off from the street. Alejandro didn't come here often—people who lived in Miramar called dollar cabs on the phone.

"I sure do miss my son. He's too busy to come visit much, of course."

Alejandro came back to the present. *Too busy to visit his own mother?*

She frowned and brushed a crumb from her blouse. "His wife says the children are too small to make the journey. And you, young man—a family? A beau? Someone to take care of you when you get home at night?"

"Me, no. I am alone."

"Well. You must be the only Cuban fellow I've met who doesn't have a girl."

"I had someone." He swallowed. "But she left me." The old woman said nothing, so he carried on. "It was supposed to be a holiday. A friend from abroad, she said. She'd known him for some time—hard to refuse. Her chance to travel and of course she would be back. She said… She said that I was intelligent enough to understand."

"But she didn't come back."

"No, she did—to say she was going to marry her friend and live with him in Munich."

"Her friend, who was he?"

"Some German. They met in a bar in Havana, one of the places tourists like to visit. I hear he is older, some kind of shopkeeper. He has nothing—nothing but the passport I don't have."

"Foolish girl… to leave you for so little. When anyone can see how much you have here."

Alejandro half-laughed, half-spat onto the dashboard. *"How much we have here?"*

"Material hardship isn't the end of the world. Selling yourself for a passport is." She pursed her lips. "You Cubans don't know the meaning of poverty. Everyone in this country eats. Sometimes I wonder just how you people feel when you reach your 'nirvana' in the States—working in factories—

chauffeurs and maids for rich people who call you 'Latino dirt'. What do you imagine—they'll give you houses and healthcare for free? The streets are paved with gold? I'll tell you now young man, if that's what you have in mind you've got it very wrong."

Alejandro had to think for a moment before replying. These foreigners who came here with all their talk confused him. He wished he could make them live like Cubans—they'd soon stop talking then.

"Everyone here eats, it is true. Everyone eats just enough so that he can live." He spoke deliberately. "He has just so much rice, beans and sugar each month from his ration book. He can't buy new clothes, can't decorate his house, which he probably shares with his mother, sister, aunts and cousins. He hasn't money to go out in the night, or buy a new dress for his wife"—he took a breath—"can't choose where he will go on holiday. And at the end of the month he must explain to the bus driver that he has nothing for the fare, and hope the driver lets him on. You and I can debate, if you like, whether we will call this a life, or just existence."

He wiped the sweat from the back of his neck with his handkerchief.

It hadn't always been like this. Once, Alejandro had believed in all the Revolution taught. It was when he tried to question that he found revolutionary zeal should stop at following the Party line. If you valued your job, your home, your child's education, you went every month to the meeting of your local Committee for the Defence of the Revolution. You attended the marches in support of Fidel, waving your Cuban flag—with or without enthusiasm. If you didn't, it was written down—your workplace kept a register—marked on your record forever.

They got you early—you sang the first songs in praise of Che at kindergarten. They chose everything for you—your school, the books you read, your hobbies, even what you were going to study at university. By the time you were an adult, it was almost impossible to think for yourself.

Alejandro had found himself longing for chaos, disorder, inequality — anything rather than life in this torpor.

La vieja was still talking. "You see only what you don't have." She swiped at a fly. "Now Brazil, that's real poverty for you. Children killing each other. Sickness. People going barefoot in the street." She took another biscuit from the pack and leaned back in her seat. "Rome wasn't built in a day, you know."

Alejandro swerved to avoid a bicycle and sounded the horn, hard. He wanted her to know how it was to try and stop your thoughts because otherwise you got so frustrated that you were driven to despair. But they never understood; these people were from another world.

There was a loud bang and the car spun to a halt. *Carajo* — not now, not a working day. Sunday was the day for bursting a tyre.

They were right in the middle of Seventh. The two of them sat for a second, staring straight ahead.

"Well! If it hasn't gone and happened again. I seem to be a curse on Cuban cars," said the old woman sitting up, her back very straight. "Come on then, we'll have to get this thing off the road." She opened her door and got out.

Alejandro followed her onto the pavement, where a knot of sympathetic bystanders had gathered.

"Señor," she was saying to a young black man in singlet and shorts, "could you help us push our car? We seem to be in some trouble."

"Claro," he said, grinning wide. He had only two front teeth, pointed like a dog's. "Dale, compañeros — let's push."

When the car was out of harm's way Alejandro opened the boot and pulled out a spanner, a jack and an oil can. Last out was the spare wheel.

"Señora, I am sorry for the disturbance. You'll get another cab, though, easily from here."

"Don't be foolish. I'm sure it won't take long," she said. "Besides, you might need some help."

Alejandro was starting to feel uncomfortable. She was attracting attention that he didn't need.

He began loosening the wheel nuts but they were stiff so he dribbled on a little oil.

"Coño!" His hand slipped and the spanner clattered to the ground.

"Here, let me do that." She took the oil can and squatted beside him. "I'll just put a little on whenever you say."

She picked up the spanner from the ground and handed it to him. Alejandro continued to loosen the nuts one by one.

Soon she wiped her forehead. The kerchief had come down slightly and a clump of white hair hung over her right cheek, which was now a livid red.

"Señora, are you very well? Because, in this heat, those not accustomed, like yourself, may start to feel a little ill."

"Yes, yes." She pushed her hair back and straightened the kerchief. "We have heat in Taos too, you know." But lines of sweat ran down her temples, and after a moment's pause, during which the only sound was the creaking of the spanner, she said: "It does seem awful hot. How about I fetch us both a cold drink? We'd surely be the better for it."

"Of course."

She stood up and made for a food stand across the street.

Alejandro wished he hadn't let her help him—he should have told her to go as soon as the trouble started. In the distance, he saw a police car. There'd be questions if they found him like this with a foreigner.

He positioned the jack under the car and raised it to touch the frame. Then he extended the jack until the burst tyre was six inches off the ground and removed the nuts from the bolts. The old wheel came away easily, like boiled chicken from the bone.

Alejandro sighed as he had a thousand times over this old heap of metal—*este carro de mierda*—and thought of how, far from making things better, the taxi had marked the beginning of the end for him and Juana; of how he'd arrive home from days sweating in the cab to see her smile distractedly, then lose herself in study again. Maybe she'd been planning her future with the German even then, he thought, kicking at a bolt.

The new wheel was stiff; he gave it a couple of whacks to get it into place and began to tighten the nuts. He caught his hand and swore. The maldito spanner, even that was useless—too large. He bit his thumb to take away the pain and tightened one last nut, wiping off excess oil with a rag. Then he lowered the jack. Now she'd go. Satisfied, he sat back on his haunches and surveyed his work.

And here was la vieja, flip-flapping along, a can of drink in each hand.

"Hey," she said from a few yards away, waving the cans in the air. "Take a break." She seemed to be swaying, walking far too quickly for this heat. As she came closer she wiped one arm across her forehead and struggled for breath. "I feel a little faint, I must sit down."

"No need to—"

Before Alejandro could finish his sentence she had crumpled to the ground. Her head hit the pavement with a crack and the cans rolled into the gutter.

He looked on in horror. Her kerchief had slipped, to reveal a temple of bluish red. One arm lay twisted behind her back, while the other was limp in front, knucklebones showing through pale white skin.

An anxious crowd gathered, throwing out advice.

"Lie her on her side!"

"No, you mustn't move her!"

"Bind up the wound!"

Her eyes were closed but she was still breathing. Alejandro checked her pulse and removed his T-shirt, rolling it into a pillow, which he put under her head. He cursed himself for having taken a tourist fare. He'd have to get her out of here quickly, before the police came—and get the car away, or he'd lose it, and his licence too.

"Find a phone and call an ambulance!" someone shouted.

No. That would be the end for him. The ambulance crew would take his licence number. He'd have to answer questions. The police would find out.

Then, thank God, a man came running from the house opposite. "Don't wait for the ambulance—the operator says there aren't any. Somebody take her to the hospital, take her now."

"I'll drive her," Alejandro said. He'd take her to his room and look after her there. She'd be all right. He was a doctor, he knew what to do.

"Here, help me get her up." He pulled the T-shirt from underneath her head and bundled her arms behind her.

They lifted the old woman into the cab and laid her across the back seat with her legs folded up against the door. Her eyes were still closed.

"Go—rápido!" The man with pointed teeth banged on the side of the car.

Alejandro pressed his thumb onto the starter button. She'd have to go, damn it, have to. The Buick gave a rattle and a cough, threw a plume of black smoke into the crowd and jerked forwards into the road.

He tore down Seventh—mercifully, the traffic was light. The sun beat onto the old woman's face through the back window—she looked okay, but her skin was bluish. Too pale. Jesus, those fair faces looked so much worse when drained of blood.

He'd have to hide her when they came to Centro Habana. Police stood on every corner there. What could he use? He grabbed at the fabric of the roof. Could he use that? What about her breathing? It was too hot to stifle her like that. Mierda! He was running with sweat, the handkerchief was soaked. This was just a faint—wasn't it? Okay, she'd banged her head but… But she was old. It could be far more serious— she might even die.

She should be in hospital where they could keep a check on her vital signs. What if her heart stopped? He wouldn't be able to save her then. *No, it would be okay.* Why did he always imagine the worst? Save yourself, he thought, digging on the accelerator. Always following the rules. Can't you think for yourself—just once? She's a tourist: she'll go back to the States, but you could lose everything.

He reached the tunnel and sped through to Vedado. On Línea, at the junction with G, he stopped at the lights. Straight ahead was the road to Centro Habana and his room. If you turned left, the road led to the hospital where he used to work.

He pictured his old ward: a long, high-ceilinged room with a row of iron beds on either side. Jorge would almost certainly be there. Jorge, Alejandro's senior by three years, had helped him through his final exams, testing him on biochemistry, endlessly patient when Alejandro needed appendectomy procedure explained for the third and fourth times. *My friend,* Jorge would say, *where have you been? We've heard nothing from you for so long.* How would Alejandro reply? What could he possibly say apart from "Luchando"?

Would he tell Jorge how Juana had left him? And the cab—how would he explain that? He probably wouldn't have to; you couldn't keep anything secret in this town.

"There's always a place for you here," Jorge had said when Alejandro left the hospital. And his reply? "It's too hard." He cringed, suddenly, at the thought. Once, he had been content. Yes, you had to be smart to get by, but he didn't lie awake bitter in the nights. When had that begun? Was it when the dollar shops arrived? When people started coming home on Saturdays with washing machines and TVs?

The lights were still red. *Change, change, change.* Why so slow? Just let him get her back to the room. He could tend to her there.

Traffic at the other side of the junction stopped. All four sides were stopped. A mother led her little girl across; they reached the kerb. The lights were green, the way down Línea was clear.

The old woman moaned.

"Quiet!" He heard his voice: it was almost a growl.

"Paul? Is that you? It's so hot in here… My head hurts. Help me, Paul… Fetch me something for my head."

He looked at her, calling for the doctor son she hardly ever saw. She was turning her head from side to side, fists jammed into the crack at the back of the seat. Sweat had plastered her hair down onto the top of her head; thin pink scalp showed through. *Dios mío.* What was he doing? Shouting at this feeble creature like a dog. He'd let her die for the sake of a taxi? A taxi that had been Juana's idea—*Juana's,* not his.

The car behind leant on its horn.

A-le-jan-dro—it meant *protector.* Some protector he was now.

The green money bag sat almost empty on the dashboard. Alejandro grabbed it and flung it from the window, then turned and drove fast towards the hospital.

LUCA'S TRIP TO HAVANA

THE SHRILL INSISTENCE of the hotel phone dragged Luca Sasso from a heavy sleep. He reached out and took a slug from last night's whiskey, which sat crystallising in a glass beside the bed. The phone fell silent.

This was his third visit here on business and each time he took the same suite at the hotel. He stared up at the ceiling, tracing patterns in the pale blue paint that seemed always to smell toxic, no matter how long ago they had put it on. At night a sulphurous smell invaded from a nearby factory, or you kept the windows shut and froze to the rattling of an ancient air-conditioner that circulated viruses and stale air.

His trousers and new Canali shirt lay where he had dropped them the night before, a mess of twisted clothes in the middle of the floor. Here and there were papers; his crocodile-skin briefcase sat open on a chair beside the desk.

The phone rang again. Let it ring, he thought, but found his hand reaching out, lifting the receiver to his ear.

"Why is your mobile off?" a voice at the other end said loudly, so that he had to hold the receiver slightly away. It was his wife, Ilene. "I've been sick with worry. For all I knew, you could have been dead."

"My dear, I was only sleeping."

Luca tried to pay attention to what his wife was saying but her voice faded out as the image rose in his mind of a rounded mulatta arse that he had admired the night before as he sat with his Cuban associate Leosbel in the hotel bar.

"Are you listening to me?" said Ilene.

"Of course, cara." He brought to mind the owner of the arse, a good-looking Cuban woman—with *muchas nalgas*, as they said here. He had seen her once before—where was it? That daffodil-yellow top... It was the morning he had arrived: she was in the lobby with a group of tourists—a guide or something like that. She had returned Luca's gaze for just a second too long, then looked away.

"Luca?" Some moments seemed to have passed without the input required of him, but Ilene was still there. "It's not too much to ask, is it? A call, a message to let us know you're all right. If you can't manage it for me ... I may be uninteresting to you now, but ... the mother of your child ... only..." The words were fading in and out. "Your daughter, at least, for her. Think of Paola."

Ilene was right. He should talk to his daughter, even from here—especially from here. His Paola. She was 17 now and beginning to spark male attention—men, not boys any more. Luca thought of the jewelled crucifix he had bought for her in the hotel's specialist gem shop. Yes, he would ask her to wear it always, for him, when he got back home.

He scratched around under his pyjama bottoms and reached for his book, which he propped against the bed covers. *Anna Karenina*—Luca enjoyed investigating the classics. It fell open at just the right page.

Ilene was still talking ... lunch with Trudi ... Via Condotti ... cocktails at the Tea Rooms because they were "so English". Then she clicked off.

He looked at his watch. Damn. Breakfast closed in half an hour and he hated doing his toilet in a rush.

A small green lizard darted onto the edge of the bed. It paused when it saw him, head cocked, completely still. Luca looked back. He understood that the creature was watching him from the way it turned its head so that both eyes faced his. He lifted one arm and cast a monster shadow over the animal; it darted for cover under the bed.

At breakfast, Luca ate from a buffet of mango and pineapple, and picked at a watery omelette. He rustled his paper, sitting behind it as if waiting for someone, to shield his embarrassment at facing the holidaying couples alone.

Ilene's voice rang in his head. *Maybe you'll behave better without Fabio,* it said. Well, maybe he would, maybe he wouldn't. God, even this far away there was no peace ... *Poor Fabio. But he brought it on himself.*

Fabio had been more than just a business partner: he had been a friend. After Fabio's death on their last trip to Cuba, Luca had thought for a few months that he would have to call the whole venture off. He just hadn't the heart to carry on. But then he decided that the best tribute to Fabio would be to pick up the baton and keep running.

And now the Cubanacán Group was almost ready to sign a contract with the firm that he and Fabio had built—to manage the hotel. There was big money to be made from tourists who expected the kind of standards that only European contacts and expertise could deliver.

He had a whole morning to kill until it was time to meet Leosbel and run through the contract. Of course there was always diving, but he couldn't face it. Luca hoisted himself into swimming trunks that almost hid his belly, which was getting too soft for his liking, and combed his hair into what he thought was a reasonably distinguished look. Then he pulled on a robe and made his way down to the lobby, where a sliding glass door led to the pool.

He lay back on a sun-lounger and opened *Anna Karenina,* but the sun was too strong. White light bounced off the pool, bleaching and glazing everything in sight. He could feel beads of sweat on his upper lip and moisture between his thighs. He put the book down.

Sun-soaked Italian girls browned their skinny legs and smoked while dark Latino boyfriends twisted restlessly beside them. The water flickered like an old TV set in the blaze.

Here and there a Cuban had somehow got into the enclosure. The sounds of a little black girl, and her mother in an electric-blue bikini, speaking Cuba's taut, half-swallowed Spanish, floated up from beside the water. The mother was probably the "sweetheart" of one of the hotel guests. Luca smiled to himself—he knew the drill. Only tourists were allowed to use the pool; all of the hotel facilities, in fact— especially the bedrooms—were out of bounds to Cubans, apart from hotel staff. It was to stop prostitution, but you could bribe in a Cuban sweetheart with a few dollar bills.

"Viejo! What's going on?" It was José, Luca's dive coach, calling from the lifeguard's hut beside the pool.

Luca waved.

"I have something for you," said José. "Come."

Luca went over and the two men shook hands. José disappeared into the hut and came out with a livid snapshot of a baby. "Say hello to Yanelis—one more since you were here last time!"

"Bonita."

"You got your eye on any baby-makers?" José winked.

Luca didn't say anything. Married men were so open about their infidelities here but it wasn't the Italian way.

In truth, there was no one worth looking at today. He glanced over at the pool—the pinkish skin of an Englishwoman with cellulite stained the white tiles at the edge of the water. The problem with European women was that they talked endlessly about sex, yet when you took them to bed they were prissy and wanted romance, like some old maiden aunt.

What he liked about Cuban women was that you didn't have to play games to get them; they could take a compliment without sneering at you as if you'd offered up your soul. He wondered where the daffodil-yellow girl was now—those nalgas! She liked him, he was sure.

A rhythmic splashing came from the pool. There was a girl in there, swimming alone, long strokes up and down in a black costume. She had done a slight dance to avoid him as she walked to the water, and there was something about the way she looked to the side as she passed, a kind of modesty, that had caught his eye. You'd never get that in a Latin girl, he thought. She must be northern—Dutch, maybe, or English.

The girl came out of the water and wrapped herself in one of the hotel's huge tangerine towels. She seemed to be hunting for something among the deckchairs.

"Can I help?" he called. "What have you lost?"

"Oh, my hat and sunglasses," she said. "They were here before and now I can't find them."

As he got up, she found them underneath a tangle of towels. Her smile was gone and she had moved towards the exit before Luca could even get near. He took his book and sat back down. He thought he caught the girl's pitying glance as she left through the sliding glass door to the side.

It was just after 11pm. Luca sat in the balcony bar, looking down at the pool. He pushed a straw around his glass: sangría, red gluey sangría—why on earth he had chosen this he did not know—with lemon and a cherry in it. He surveyed the line of beautiful Cuban girls at the bar. At home these girls would be with young handsome studs, but it wasn't like that here—you didn't get the attitude: *Yeah, what do you want from me?* Here, it was as if they were waiting—waiting just for you.

But it wasn't the same without Fabio. They would have had fun together, rating the girls, making a game out of who could pull the best. Just a couple more days and he would fly back to Rome, Ilene and the sweaty office at the Piazza di Pavia. He let out a deep sigh.

Then he saw her—the daffodil-yellow girl. She was sitting at a table nearby, yellow top painted onto polished brown skin, her muscles strong and defined. She was smiling, and leaning into the table, which she shared with another Cuban woman and a tourist. Luca could tell that the man was a tourist because the two women spoke slowly, and repeated Spanish phrases over and over. She didn't want the man, Luca calculated—her manner was more polite than flirtatious—but she seemed to be enjoying herself anyway. Her smile was one of genuine pleasure; she wasn't sluttish, just deliciously sexy, like a panther.

The bar would be closing soon—how would he play it? You found three types of girl in a Cuban bar: the prostitute, in and out in an hour; the jinetera—she'd stay for a few days, take a little money, give a little love; and the sweetheart, who would never want to leave. This girl looked like the sweetheart type, probably hoping to snag a foreign husband and a better life abroad.

Luca didn't want a sweetheart, but maybe she could do with a few dollars or some nice new clothes. What Cuban couldn't? He'd have to play it down, though: the nicer ones didn't like to feel bought. But they all liked passion—it was in their blood.

She got up and walked towards the bar. The barman brushed her shoulder with his fingers and she laughed.

Luca drew himself up from the chair. He smoothed his hair and moved to the other side of a pillar where she was leaning, her arm casually against it, wrist bared to the night. His bulk dwarfed her—not just her height, but her frame, which he now realised was more fragile than it had first appeared.

She didn't look at him, but Luca could tell that she was interested, in that way women have of letting you know with a sideways glance, as if caught off-guard. He pressed his forearm against her wrist, crushing it into the pillar. She let him, then pulled away.

He thought that he had mistaken her, but then she turned her face up to his. He looked back hard and made his stare say *I want you*, as he'd seen the Cubans do. For a moment, he believed it was not interest he saw in her eyes, but surprise, or even fear—then he reminded himself that this wasn't a cock-tease Italian he was dealing with: sex was what they wanted, these Cuban women. They started around 11, like riding a bike, and hopped on and off whenever necessary after that.

Just as he opened his mouth to speak, Luca realised that she was ogling some young black guy across the room—he looked like one of the kitchen staff, playing table tennis in only his vest. Why did they always have such effortlessly rippling torsos, these Cubans, when there was hardly a gym on the block?

Luca threw a ten-dollar bill down next to the half-finished glass of sangría and went back to his room.

The following day he went from Vedado to Miramar and back again, talking with stonemasons, painters, electrical suppliers and telecoms engineers, working out how far the firm could deliver on plans for the hotel refurbishment using local trade. By the time evening came, Luca was glad to shower and lie down in his room. He plugged in his mobile and found there were several messages from the office, and two from Ilene, whom he would call later. The heat here was worse than Rome.

He decided to have a quiet night in the balcony bar. She wasn't there and he couldn't work out if he was glad.

The next night he went to a salsa club with Leosbel and some Cubans from the hotel management group.

The night after that he was back in the balcony bar.

She was there with a glass in her hand. She wasn't alone, though—she was talking to the head porter, Alexei. When Alexei saw Luca, a flash of irritation crossed his face, but Luca couldn't work out why. Alexei had a wife, who was beautiful, and a kid. He couldn't be jealous. They sat with him sometimes in the bar during the day.

Luca picked a table and pretended to read the menu; he studied her from behind it.

She saw him and said something to Alexei, who glanced over at Luca and shook his head, then she came and perched on the chair next to his.

"You are alone?" she said.

"No—yes—"

" —here on business."

Luca nodded.

She touched the cuff of his Canali shirt. "This is the Italian style?"

"This? Yes." He was glad he'd had it laundered.

"Alexei told me you are from Rome. But I guessed it anyway—because you are so *elegante*."

Luca lowered his voice. "Why was he looking at me like that? Is he jealous?"

"He sees many extranjeros here, dipping in and out of our hearts—"

" —but you Cubans are all heart."

"For someone decente, sí—una relación decente. But… the foreign men, you know, sometimes they take our hearts too soon."

He wondered if he was the first visitor she'd got caught up with. She didn't seem the jinetera type.

He found that her name was Ella and she had worked in the hotel for two months. This was her first job after leaving university, where she had studied maths.

"What do you think about Cuba?" she said.

"I like it. Especially the pretty girls."

"But Italian girls they are beautiful! Like the Vogue magazine."

"Yes, but" —he reached forward and touched her knee— "they're not *caliente* like the Cuban ladies."

She stayed completely still, neither moving from his touch nor responding to it. "It is true—we are muy intenso. But we are women too. I think not so different? We need also to be loved." She smoothed a curl at his temple with her fingers, so delicately it was almost not a come-on.

"Your skin is like silk," he said.

Alexei was eyeing them—he and a bunch of hip young Cubans by the bar.

"They are just boys," she said, following Luca's gaze, "with nothing to do. In your country success takes time, because you have where to go in your life. It takes time to grow into something that is strong—like a big rooted tree."

He found that he could not look at her. *You're worrying again,* he heard Fabio's voice say. *Why don't you have some fun? What harm can it do?*

"Here, everything is por interés," she said. "One day you meet, the next day you are married, and the next one divorced."

"I'd marry you in a heartbeat." He enclosed her hand with his. "*Sei bellissima.*"

She pulled her hand away. "Not here."

"Why not?" He knew why, but said it anyway.

"We are not supposed to—hotel workers with the guests."

"But I can't help myself. You make me want you." For some reason he thought of his first girlfriend, Alba. He leaned in. "My little Alba."

"What are you saying?"

"She is the heroine of a very famous story—in fact, the novel I'm reading—a beautiful woman like you, who wanted to be free." He did not think of looking away. "Let's go somewhere else."

"I can't, not tonight. My little brother is alone."

"Call him." Luca held out his mobile.

"We do not have a telephone in the house—but tomorrow also I am here."

"Tomorrow I leave for Rome."

She sighed and touched something at her neck. "Qué pena!" When she moved her hand away, Luca saw that it was a crucifix.

"Till next time, then." He stood. She seemed to be waiting for something. She held her face up and Luca remembered— the polite way to say goodbye to a woman here was with a peck on the cheek. He turned without kissing her and walked to the door.

He made his way down the spiral staircase from the balcony bar and along the path beside the pool. The path led to the hotel lobby, then back to his room. He paused at the lifeguard's hut and leaned into the open doorway, watching the city and the hustlers at street level below. So that one had got away. Resistance wouldn't have put Fabio off—he'd just have gone in harder for the kill.

Then he saw her. She was coming along the path, treading carefully on the dark night cobbles. She looked out over the water, and the moon caught her eyes and the tops of her gold sandals.

"Hey," he said, almost too quietly, from the shadows.

She turned, searching the dark, and before the moon silhouetted her out completely, the half-light held her vivid, open face.

"Come here a minute," he said.

She hesitated. "What do you want?"

"Nothing — just to talk."

The tops of her arms had goose bumps, and wind from the sea flapped at the bottom of her damson skirt. He held out his hand. She looked around, as if to check whether anyone was watching, and walked towards the doorway of the hut.

As soon as their fingers touched, Luca pulled. They triangled over the threshold. He pivoted her round until her back was against the wall and pushed, a hand on her shoulder, up against the concrete. He put his lips on hers; their teeth clashed and he corkscrewed his tongue down her throat.

She pressed him away. Her black eyes were feral.

"*No,*" she said. "I want to know you first."

He released her.

"Listen," he said. "We don't have to do anything, we can just talk." Like this it was even more exciting than other nights, with other girls, in the room — but he would have to slow it down. "Don't spoil your face by frowning. Come on — *amore.*" He thought he saw a flicker in her eyes, just the beginning of a smile — Alba again. "You know, this isn't the first time I've stayed here, and it won't be the last. I want to get to know you."

"Not the last?"

"Yes. We're taking over the hotel contract, so I'll be back."

She let her shoulders drop.

"You see? No need to worry." Luca caught her wrist. He

tried to kiss her again but she twisted her face away. He fixed his arms around her—he could feel how taut her muscles were. These mulattas were like oxen, bred for work.

"Kiss me," he said.

"No! Déjame." She tried to pull away. "No lo quiero así!"

"Shhhh." He put a hand over her mouth. "I know you want me. There's no more time."

A footstep came from the path.

She squealed.

"*Quiet*," he said. "They'll hear you."

He kneed her legs apart but she forced them back. *Puttana*. What did she want? He put both hands on her hips and pressed so that she scissored backwards against a cupboard. The shiny fabric of her skirt rode up beneath his hands, damp in the heat, and her knees buckled. She was making small noises—mewling whines—lust, at last. Funny how their enjoyment often sounded like pain. He pinned her against the cupboard and—she seemed to be getting into it—felt her tongue move against his as he tore through flimsy nylon and lace.

Naked she was no longer tempting, just a mountain of flesh to be screwed. He spread her on the floor beneath him. A bolt of moonlight cut her neck; he caught a glint of something—the crucifix. He pulled it round to her back, closed his eyes and pushed inside hard. She juddered in time, quiet now. Her face was turned to the side but it was better that way; Ilene's close-up crazy knowing had got to freaking him out. Luca strained his neck, his grunts and eyes far beyond her frozen stare until he came—*Alba, Alba* in the dark beyond his sight.

Seconds in the stillness then Alba was gone. There was no Alba, just a dead dog beneath him. He shrank into a ball and pressed his sight black with a fist.

There was nothing but the sound of the street.

She put a hand on his arm. It lay there like a dead thing.

"Look at me," she said.

He placed her hand on the floor.

"Why won't you look at me?"

He closed his eyes.

"Do you have a wife?"

They never gave you a break. Not Alba, not Ilene—not even this mulatta here. He pushed at her hip. "You like it from the other side?"

She shook him off.

"What? What's the matter?"

She stood up. "You are a coward … sin vergüenza." He just lay there. Her voice came from somewhere above him: "You have a black hole for a heart."

Luca slept a restless sleep. The telephone was silent. He woke halfway through the night and saw the lizard, illuminated by a shaft of light from the moon. It ran onto the sideboard, pausing when it saw him, head cocked, completely still. He could have crushed the beast with his fist. It turned its head so that both eyes pointed towards his; he slammed his arm into the air and it darted beneath the bed.

In the morning Luca dressed and ate and turned his thoughts to work. Over coffee he prepared a report of the previous day's meeting with Cubanacán, talking carefully into his Dictaphone so that Stefania could type it up at the office. He went through the proposals agreed, matching each one to plans made with the partners in Rome, costing out the price differences and justifying extra expense where he thought it necessary to secure the hotel bid.

The plane was due to leave at five. He packed his case, then stood at the window and thought of Fabio—Fabio, who had gone on a night dive without ropes and lost his way in a set of labyrinthine caves beneath the Cuban sea. They had found him with his arms folded across his chest as if he had not fought death—maybe even welcomed it.

He saw her as he checked out of the hotel. She was standing in the lobby at the head of a group of new arrivals next to a sign that said: *Tours to Habana Vieja Here.*

"Hi!" he said. "How are you?"

She fixed him with blank eyes. "Señor?"

I NEVER SEE THEM CRY

WHEN JABAITO SAYS, "My family loves you, of course, because I love you," I am entranced. *Of course*—no one at home would ever say that, even if you'd known them for years. I imagine disappearing with Jabaito into the countryside, and now it is really happening: we are going to La Bajada, where his family lives.

Jabaito's village is so remote that the newspaper has to be delivered by plane—five hours by a rough road after the autopista stops. The communist daily, *Granma*, gets dropped into a field at lunchtime every day.

We come off the highway and take a smaller road. This one is almost empty, just people walking along—walking and walking because there's no other way to get to where you're going—or waiting, just hordes of people sitting on the sides of the road looking as if they've been there for hours and expect to be for many more. We pass a truck full of green bananas, and a man selling cheese and guava on a plate, standing by the side of the road holding up just one plate of it. Then we come to a valley of palm trees bathed in cloud and it starts to rain.

Jabaito has told me, and I sort of believe him, that he will not go away. My mother died soon after we met and I fought in his arms in the dark till he made me quiet by saying: "I will be there. When your father is gone, you will still have me."

The roads get smaller and smaller till finally we limp through puddles down a street of brown boxes where families sit outside on porches and the sun steams dry the trees. A sign by the side of the road says: *Aquí no se rinde nadie*—Here, nobody surrenders. We pull up at a house with brown shutters. An old man sits on a wooden chair on the porch next to a pile of broken shoes. The door is open. A large woman in a pink top stained with dirt comes out.

"Sarah, this is my great aunt Edita," says Jabaito, pushing me in front of him. "And this"—pointing to the old man—"is her husband Pápio." The old man shuffles forward. He is very thin and his belly wrinkles over the top of his trousers; the fly is gaping open.

Inside the house Fidel is talking on TV but no one is watching. Black and white lines rise permanently across the set. The room is almost bare—a cement floor and a couple of chairs. Pictures of a voluptuous girl in a Scarlett O'Hara dress cling bravely to the peeling walls. Jabaito disappears into the kitchen, where a large pot of rice is just visible cooking on the stove, and starts talking to several people in there at the top of his voice. I've never heard him talk so much before—at parties in Havana he'll just stand to the side, looking incredibly handsome in a white shirt and chinos, getting progressively, quietly drunk.

I sit on a wicker couch next to the woman in the stained top and begin telling her about my course at the University of Havana.

"What is it exactly that you do there, dear?" she says.

"I'm studying Spanish literature."

"Ah yes, Jabaito explained it to us. You met in the square outside the university, when he was waiting for a bus."

Pápio sits in a rocker nearby, an amused half-smile on

his face, head turning like a puppet's on a pole.

Edita begins recounting the quinceañera of her granddaughter Melba—the one who pouts at us from the wall.

"I had no daughters," she says. "I brought her up from chiquitica as if she were my own."

She pulls out an old plastic photo album. In some of the pictures Melba is wearing a white bridal gown almost to the floor, over patent leather shoes and frilly socks, smiling radiantly from under a curly mane. In others she is crouching down in black, looking up at the camera as if it were her lover. One has her sitting astride a motorbike, the background streaked out to a blur.

A final shot shows Melba surrounded by people. "That is her mother," says Edita, pointing to a small woman at the edge of the crowd. "She came because—well, I suppose she came to the party because she *is* her mother."

I try to imagine having a mother who is alive but who never comes to my house.

"Isn't she lovely?" Edita's body is turned almost entirely towards me. My Spanish is quite good now, and I try to talk enthusiastically about the photographs, despite needing to go to the toilet. "Qué linda! Qué linda!" I say over and over again.

A man comes through the front door, wearing Elvis glasses and blue trousers, his chest bare. He fires something out in rapid Spanish and continues to the kitchen.

"Sarah, in your country do you celebrate the quinceañera?" Edita asks.

"Not really," I say. "We don't have a special party when a girl turns 15. In England it would be more when she's 18."

"England…" Pápio nods from his chair. "England—they say that's near to Spain." Someone has slung a towel over his gaping fly.

I feel bit light-headed after the journey—hours stuffed into the back of a gasoline-leaking car. It's a strange feeling: here and not here.

"Please. El baño." I say.

The toilet has no seat and there are squares of *Granma* speared to the back of the bathroom door on a nail. I place my roll of two-peso paper by the side of the bowl and wash my hands with water that comes in a trickle from the tap, using a dented aluminium cup that sits on the floor. A basket of screwed-up newspaper stands under the sink, covered by cardboard cut into a disk to fit.

When I emerge, there is another man in the room, leaning against the door.

"He is my other son, Heberto," says Edita. The man grins at me and comes over. There is a big pus-filled lump on the side of his face. "The carnival," he explains. "I have grown a boil from all the partying—I must have two injections in my backside to make it go away. They're going to lance it soon."

He bends onto one knee and takes my hand. I feel his warm, sticky skin and kind words.

"Sarah wants to know why you are so fat," says Edita, even though I haven't said anything, and Heberto smiles, patting the sides of a pillow belly that stands out from the front of his pitch-black torso, oiled and shiny in the heat.

I am dozing in a lime-blue room at the front of the house. Heberto's room. Brown louvred shutters open to the street; the windows have no glass. As people pass I can see their faces, lit by the moon; there is nothing between me and them except the air.

The family is sitting in the main room but I can hear everything that is happening—the smallest thing dropped or moved, every voice.

On the beaten-up dresser stands a voluptuous woman

carved out of wood. She has big hips and small breasts—
like Alma, the one Jabaito brought me when we first met.
I thought I'd never seen anything more beautiful, that he'd
carved it specially for me, but then I discovered that they
churn them out by the dozen in his village—a "negocio"—
and flog them to tourists in Havana for $20 each.

Officially you're not allowed to trade, but in Cuba
everyone has to "resolver".

Resolver means "to get by"—to find a way round the
hundreds of restrictions on your life, get food and all the
things you need to survive. You just have to make sure you're
not caught—which can happen easily through someone you
know. Jabaito's neighbour is in the secret police and they're
always careful not to talk too loudly in case he hears. But he's
their friend as well—he comes round all the time.

I can't stop scratching: my arms are itchy and sweaty
and covered in bites. This bed is so close to the walls that it
almost touches the shutters. Everyone can see me lying here;
they see every move I make.

In London, no one looks at you at all. You could be see-
through, a ghost. I remember going for a walk once, in the
park—a summer morning, with the sun shining and the
lawns all dry. I smiled at the people who passed to see if
they'd answer but no one did.

Fidel's voice issues from every TV on the street. He has
been talking all afternoon, flickering from the family's black-
and-white set. Earlier, we all crowded round it. Fidel seemed
emotional—his voice cracked, then Heberto shouted, "Go
on! Go on!" as the picture cut to the front of a huge crowd
that was watching Fidel speak. A man hesitated, then peeled
himself from the mass and rushed towards Fidel; others
followed.

We had all hurried to watch this but I didn't understand
why. Heberto explained: Fidel had fainted—fallen down
in front of the crowd—but was back on his feet after five

minutes. Well again! El Líder was strong—in his eighties but strong as an ox, and nothing could take him down.

The scene was repeated throughout the day on TV.

Jabaito's cousin wears Elvis glasses all the time and speaks like a rapid-fire gun. His teeth show white and sometimes he chews a straw. "I pick Ingleesh! … Pik In*gleesh*? Pik In*gleesh*?" he likes to say.

Marta, a little girl of two in electric pink shorts, lives next door. Marta has her own purple chair, which she drags over from her house. Elvis tells her to sit with us, but it's her mami that she wants. Marta wants her *mami*, and mami isn't home.

Jabaito leans in to ask her for a kiss. She won't do it. Papi gave her a 10-centavos coin and she's got it in her ear. "Dame un beso," says Jabaito. We all wait, and she does.

I bathe before dinner using a tiny tub and a tin cup. "That water is for us both," says Jabaito. "Rain from a drum on the roof." Above the tub is a ripped-off shower head with a wick like a camping stove. "That used to be the shower but it's broken," says Jabaito. "They are very poor."

I wash using the tin cup and a new bar of orange soap, in my chancletas, sliding along the blue-tiled bathroom floor. I study the toilet with no seat; the squeezed-out toothpaste tubes with no name—only silver foil; the brown and green bottles on the shelf; and half a broken mirror in its frame. The curtain for the shower seems very old. I think it has mould spots on it but then I see they are the markings of a long-gone pattern. Everything is clean.

To dry, I lie on the bed—my bites are too itchy to rub with a towel. Jabaito is ironing his best white trousers and a pale lemon shirt because later, after dinner, we are going out por la calle. Jabaito is very thin. Since he lost his job at the factory his bones stick out more; his torso is only insides covered by skin.

A horse trots past pulling a cart behind it. The TV booms

from next door, where Marta is settled in her little purple chair, with a teddy, on the porch.

I still think, sometimes, that my mother will return.

Supper is outside at the back; we sit at a table under the eaves of the house. I'm still damp and the air is thick. Jabaito's cousin Cheddy is with us; they both wear white trousers with white vests tucked in. No one here wears shirts in the house—they're just for best. Jabaito's lies ready now on the bed in the lime-blue room at the front corner of the house.

On the table are numerous paper plates, set out specially for us by Elvis, who has only one eye. He looms over us during the meal, encouraging, tasting, directing.

"Have you ever tried crocodile?" he asks. "Listen, you can try some and if you don't like it we will give it to Cheddy and Jabaito—but you will. You will like it. It's a great delicacy!"

I eat the four pieces of crocodile meat with lime juice that sit on my plate. They taste like a strong fish.

"You must try every dish! Something from every plate." His breath is hot on my back. "Who was the cook? It was me!"

There is cucumber—sliced and peeled—in lemon juice, cucumber—unpeeled —with salt, thick wedges of pineapple, fish fried to a crisp, black beans and rice.

I pick up a piece of fish.

"Where did you get that?" Jabaito asks Elvis. "Fishing's been forbidden for months now."

Elvis winks and throws a shifty look at the garden fence, as if the neighbours might be listening. "I know a man."

When we were getting ready, Elvis could hear our disco music and would break into a small groove every now and then. His smile slipped out of him sideways. You'd not know his tenderness from the barking, till later—like when he bent down over Marta to enfold her and his smiling teeth showed, one eye warm, the other an inflamed purple absence.

"Fish!" Cheddy suddenly says. Until now he's been too busy spooning food into his mouth to speak. "I'm glad Sarah's here."

I didn't realise fish was anything special—I thought they could take it from the sea whenever they liked. "Just one piece for me," I say.

Jabaito laughs. "It's just one piece for everyone, Sarah."

My thighs are stuck to the plastic chair and the strange feeling from earlier has not lifted, as if I'm falling ill in some as yet undefined way. Cheddy sits in the chair opposite me, his back low, so that he is half-lying, his long brown legs open in a V. He keeps a can of Cachito in his hand, rolling it back and forth from one gold-ringed finger to another. Every now and then he catches my eye. I don't know him that well, but Cheddy's eyes are kind.

Nieves arrives—Cheddy's girlfriend. Her little flat-chested form suits his because he is little too, like a size 1 version of his brother Heberto. She is wearing a long silky dress; perfume rises from her shoulders like steam. Her hair is smoothed into a bun with silvery beads knotted through the sides.

"Oh you smell good—what's that beautiful smell?" Elvis sniffs around her slim brown arms.

She smiles tightly.

"Heh heh, a dress!" he laughs, big over her. She is slight and her face buttoney like Cheddy's. It doesn't move much. "A dress is easy! Not like trousers when you have to unbutton them. A dress you can just pull it up and … heh heh!" Elvis winks at Cheddy, mimes pulling a dress over the head, and cracks up.

Jabaito smirks and sniggers slightly. I try, and fail, to meet his eye. I've never seen him like this before.

Nieves looks annoyed.

"Oh come on!" Elvis holds a hand out to give her five but she turns her head away.

The next morning, as we sit and eat our breakfast, I know I am not well. We are in the yard behind the house amid the flies and bins and metal bits. Elvis is reading the communist youth daily, *Juventud Rebelde*, and *Granma* at the same time. Jabaito perches with Cheddy on a chair, chewing his way through bread and milk. The heat is prickling in.

I am tired and irritated and have nothing to say. I need some time alone but I am surrounded by people. Only Heberto isn't here—where has he gone? Last night we came home to find him sleeping on the wicker couch, but now he is nowhere to be seen. I push down panic that rises at the thought of sickness in the seat-less toilet and the heat, surrounded by strangers, never alone.

Last night we gathered in the town square. Loud music came from a mobile bar in an old wrecked bus. The girls were all done up perfectly—hair in flowers and bows, long dresses to the ground and platform shoes, or short ones that covered almost nothing. Boys were in white, hair gelled, even the small ones not much grown. They sat round tables drinking beer, like we do at home but quiet and well-behaved. It was like a set for a music video, everyone waiting for action while the director checks the lights.

I walked between Cheddy and Jabaito and suddenly felt that I had never met them before. I am a stranger, I thought.

But it wasn't true, because clearly they knew me—soft and naked, a hermit crab without a shell.

In the yard, they are all staring. What is wrong, everyone wants to know, asking me to repeat my symptoms several times. A discussion breaks out as to what is best to do. Everyone has a different opinion but finally a consensus is reached: Edita will take me to see the doctor as soon as they have finished their meal.

Jabaito brings me a green parrot from next door, perched on his finger. I tell him I like the parrot and he says I should take one home with me when I go back to England. "You can hide it in your handbag," he says. "I know a man who sells little ones, when they're still babies."

"You're not allowed to take animals on the plane," I say.

He looks doubtful.

"No one will see it if you hide it in your handbag," he says.

The doctor lives in a smart house up the street, just beyond the Seventh Day Adventist church, where a freshly painted swinging sign informs us: *Jesus — God loved the world so much that he gave it his Only Son.*

White shutters are almost closed so I think there's no one home, but Heberto answers the door. I can't work out why he's here, though Edita doesn't seem surprised. He leads us through dark plum corridors to the garden, where a blue-eyed kitten sits at the end of a rope and a blood-orange parrot grips the bars of its cage.

The doctor's house is so plush. Where did he get it all? I've never seen such luxury in Cuba before: fresh lilac paint, not the usual peeling lime, rugs on the floor, colour photographs in ornate frames — one shows a middle-aged man with olive skin smiling over a brood of blond children, and I remember that it was the whites who fled the Revolution; they meant to come back after but weren't allowed. Now they live in Miami and send over money to relatives who stayed.

Edita creaks into a rocker on the patio while Heberto goes back to shovelling earth on a plot of yellow flowers. Maybe he works here, I think. He picks up the spade, shovels, goes into the shed, then comes back out and shovels again. He does everything very slowly, thinking each action through before he makes a move. A cloud of flies buzzes round a dish of corn, and a mango bangs down from a tree, bringing a pig and a swarm of chicks in a race for food.

The doctor arrives, breathing hard, his temples running with sweat. He's been visiting a patient and heard we needed him through Elvis, on the street. He sits heavily in a chair across the table.

"So, my dear," he says in a loud voice. "What is it you are feeling?"

"I feel pain here"—I point between my legs—"and a burning."

"And you feel itching, don't you?" prompts Edita.

Heberto stands a few feet away, leaning on a spade, his head to one side.

"I see," says the doctor. "And is the itching on the *inside* or the *outside*?"

I glance over at Heberto, but he doesn't move.

"The inside." I tear the words slowly from my mouth. "But it's not itching, it's pain—and pain when I pass water too."

"You have cystitis," says the doctor. "Nothing to worry about. And thrush too, probably." He scratches down a fistful of words onto what seem to be scraps of paper but later turn out to be prescription forms. "Here—I'll give you something for the pain. It will neutralise the acid. Then you must wash twice a day with bicarbonate of soda in water—two spoons a litre. Boil the water first."

"Shouldn't I take the bicarbonate by mouth? I normally take it by mouth."

"No, no." He laughs. "Topical application is what you need. Taking it up here"—he points to his mouth—"is not going to help you down there, is it?" He laughs again.

"These are tablets for thrush." He dashes down something else and I reach for the pieces of paper but he hands them to Heberto. "You may find them at the pharmacy. Go there now. If not, try the hospital tomorrow." The doctor turns to me: "It's nothing to worry about. You'll be yourself again tomorrow. Really, it's nothing at all."

The pain is an ice-cold sword that defies the languid heat. As we say goodbye, I try to look grateful but it is a sour little smile that turns the corners of my mouth.

Edita appears not to notice. As we make our way home she dawdles, calling out greetings to the people we meet: "María! Cómo anda?" — "Eh Omar, la familia?" — she takes his hand — "Sí, Nelsa, dime!"

Just as we reach the house Edita grasps my arm and says, "Sarah, I want you to meet Marta's grandmother, Odanai."

She knocks at the neighbour's, and when there is no reply pushes open the door. Marta sits in her purple chair sucking on mashed platano from a plastic cup. She looks up at us and continues eating. Then a tiny shining woman shuffles across the polished floor. She has dark brown skin, and white hair combed across a fragile scalp; eyes like marbles strain from her skull. Marta's grandmother, Odanai.

Her body makes me hurt to look; every movement causes her pain. Her arms swing from their sockets like the bones in a dug-up cavewoman's leathery skin, but each piece of her clothing is immaculate: polished lace-up shoes, tawny skirt, the freshest white short-sleeved blouse.

"Where are you from, mi hijita?" she says.

She searches the space in front of me with her eyes. They are almost translucent. "Why are you here?"

She lifts one hand to my cheek; I bring mine up to meet it. I feel the bones, and skin like parchment that might crumble to the touch.

Edita lays me down on Heberto's bed in the lime-blue room. There is no avoiding the inquisitive eyes of the town. Whichever way I turn, somebody can see — but other than closing the shutters, which makes it so hot I can hardly breathe, there is nothing to be done.

Passing faces meet my gaze, a small child playing on a porch across the way catches my eye, and later, Jabaito's finger through the shutters pokes me out of a hazy sleep.

The mattress has lumps on it. Springs have escaped the casing, but as I lie on my back the pain rips me more than the naked metal. I touch the corners of my mouth and find them scabby with the beginning of cold sores. I want to stamp and cry but I don't because here, people don't cry. Here, they "aguantan"—hold it in.

People get drunk and fight but I never see them cry.

Heberto is the first to come back in. I open my eyes to see the whites of his as he stands there, skin oiled and shining. He looks for a while, saying nothing. His eyes are very open, still, a question in themselves.

"How do you feel?" He comes closer to the bed, one eyebrow slightly raised.

"Better than before."

"Did you wash yourself with the doctor's water?" I'm surprised to find that I don't mind this—it is said with innocence and I answer straight. He nods and leaves the room.

Horses trot past the window, pulling carts. The sound is like rain on the roof when you're sleeping.

"She says she hasn't washed herself yet but she'll do it when she takes a shower," I hear him shout. The family must be in the yard. Maybe they are cleaning rice for supper, picking out the stones and dirt.

It makes me jump to hear the state of my cleanliness announced to the house. I sit up and look around me. The street is empty—no one to see the blood rush to my face.

This is the bargain, I decide—what you give up for being held.

Heberto returns a few minutes later with an aluminium tray containing plates of meat, rice and sweet potato.

He stands by the side of the bed. I eat slowly and he watches me curiously. After a while he goes out.

I am just tucking into the sweet potatoes when I look up and see him there again. He seems to want to talk.

"It's funny, you being here in La Bajada—just as if I were in your house in London," he says. "How long is the flight to London?"

"Ten hours."

"Ten." His face is big and soft and shows each thought as it surfaces in his mind. "And England—is that somewhere near to Spain?"

"Somewhere near." I chew and a picture comes into my head of Heberto bent on one knee, holding my hand when I first arrived.

"Do you like pork?" he inquires as I cut into the meat.

My energy is returning. "I like everything," I say. "But there are two things here that I can not eat."

He looks interested so I carry on.

The first is a soapy-tasting potato thing called malanga, the second the mamey. The mamey is praised for its beauty—"Estás linda como el mamey!" men will call after a particularly luscious Cubana as she passes them on the street. But the mamey is disturbing: on first seeing its nut-like cover open to perfect flamingo flesh I thought it would be delicious, then waxy avocado meat confused my tongue with the wrong kind of sweet and I hated that. Who wants a sweet avocado? It's like strawberry-flavoured steak.

"Ah, the malanga." Heberto nods. "The malanga is a kind of meat." He falls silent. I am eating the rice now and he watches me carefully.

The sun is going down. Edita comes in and turns on the

light. It broadcasts us through open shutters to the darkness beyond.

"How do you feel, mamita?" She looks at me from the foot of the bed.

My neck is bent awkwardly against the headboard.

She comes closer, right next to the bed now in a yellow plastic apron, one side down to reveal a large breast loose under her dress.

"Yo la creé." She points to Melba's hair ribbons on the dresser. "I tell her—speak to her—I try to form her as we talk, and I tell her, 'Just because your friend has a top that cost fifteen dollars, you don't need to sell yourself to get one. You can wait until we can buy you one—from your grandfather mending shoes.'"

Melba does not give anything away with her eyes. She comes and goes in a plump silence, smooth along the streets, carrying her baby-pink bag for school. But those fat thighs can tempt from under her mustard-yellow uniform skirt. Whatever Edita says, Melba is from a different generation— one that will ride a tourist's back if that is what it takes.

"Respect. There is something more valuable than money, and that is respect." Edita has large teeth with gaps, and insistent almond eyes. "If a Cuban steals from his neighbour, a compañero will come to him and say: 'Brother, why are you stealing from your friend? Can't you see, you are stealing from yourself—from the fathers of the Revolución?'"

Heberto enters with authority, confident now in his role of nurse, and moves towards the fan on the other side of the bed. He grasps it with both hands and snaps it round to blow air straight on me, then he pads out.

"My family came from the Congo." Edita swats a fly from her brow with the yellow plastic apron. "Before the Revolución we were nothing. There was no education for us blacks back then. We could not study. We could not work. My mother taught me to read at night by the lamp at the back.

The only jobs we could do were as domestics—or worse—and now we do everything. Every job is open to us now." She moves closer, looking right into my eyes. "I am very militant. I am the head of the Unidad Zonal. The Revolución gave us everything. Before, there was racism, but every person has the right to enjoy equally the fruits of our world, whether his skin is black like mine"—she taps her forearm—"or white like yours"—she points to mine.

People are usually hidden. I can not see them, no matter how I try. But Edita is luminous, a face that can not hide.

"Now you feel better," she says. "I am like your mother. We have been talking and you forget."

As soon as it is known that the worst has passed, everyone crowds into the lime-blue room. Heberto and Cheddy stand at the foot of the bed, Edita and Jabaito sit beside me. Only Pápio remains outside, gazing dreamily at the world from his rocker on the porch.

Elvis brandishes a wire egg-cutter and a half-sliced egg.

"Look! I bought this yesterday," he says. The egg-cutter is made of green plastic. He leaves the room and returns with another egg-cutter still in its cardboard package. "For you! I bought three of them—the other one will be for my girlfriend."

Melba wanders in. She threads a scarlet ribbon into her hair for the evening, combing and twisting and watching herself in the mirror as we talk.

I'm not naked any more—or maybe I am, but being held.

It is morning and the early horses are trotting past. In the night, mosquitoes bit me but I wrapped myself in the vinyl sheet with blue flowers on it. The mattress coughed up its broken springs; Jabaito and I pressed them down under a green blanket. "My son is so fat!" said Edita—Heberto had moulded a curve into the bed that toppled us towards its centre.

Cocks crow here all morning. Bicycles ring past the window. Only 6am but people stream past to field and school on foot and horse and many bikes.

It is clean cool morning and I love the day. The words trip off me, they peel away easily like skins of the onion and I feel well.

Jabaito is awake. He is watching old black-and-white baseball on the TV. Edita comes in, stray hairs and a white gown for the night. My dreams were so big.

I feel the first stirrings of heat through the shutters. An orange glow on the horizon, and a moped splutters past. The dread memory of pain.

The heat will come.

SABBATICAL

"This is the house," said the driver, pulling the cab to a halt in front of a wide double door. The street was dark, even though they were in the middle of Havana; the outlines of the building came through the trees, lit from within by a dull glow.

"Come," he said, taking Carol's bags. "Follow me."

They climbed a staircase to the third floor, where an old lady with ginger hair stood outside a door on the landing. She was tiny, grinning up at Carol, an oil lamp in one hand.

"I am Telma," she said. "And you must be Carol, Emily's friend. Come in—I'll take you to your room." She grasped Carol's hand and pulled her through to the parlour of the apartment; the walls were a pale, minty blue and it was old, like a hotel. A large fan sat silent in the middle of the ceiling.

The old lady led Carol up a narrow flight of stairs to a room that lay among a nest of aerials on the roof. "Do forgive me," she said. "We don't normally live like this in the darkness, but there's been trouble with the current. Wait—I'll fetch you some light." She disappeared with the lamp, leaving Carol alone in the gloom.

As her eyes grew used to the dark, Carol saw that she was standing in the middle of a small, low-ceilinged room, lit from a skylight by the moon. There was a little bed with a wooden shelf above it, a telephone and a chest of drawers. On her left, through a low arch, there was a shower room and a door to the roof, which looked onto a balcony below.

She rolled her face in the warm, damp air and gazed up at the sky; even though it was past ten, the heat lay humid on her like a fog. It was quiet—just some voices and the clatter of pots and pans as dinner was served next door.

Telma reappeared.

"We've run out of candles—here, I'll leave this on the table so you can see to unpack your things." She put down the lamp.

"Won't you need some light?"

"No, dear, we're used to doing without. Come and find me when you're ready—I'll be waiting for you downstairs. You can have something to eat."

Carol pulled off her clothes. Only a trickle of water came from the shower, and it was cold, but she did her best to freshen up. She opened one of the suitcases—so much stuff! For now, she took out just the essentials: books, tea and muesli for tomorrow's breakfast. She arranged the books on the shelf—*Moon Guide to Cuba*, detective novels, and *Buddhist Boot Camp*—next to a fat ceramic woman with enormous lips who was smoking a cigar.

Downstairs, Telma was sitting in a rocking chair by a casement window open to the street. A dining table was set for one, with a bowl of rice and what looked like fried bananas. The old lady told Carol to sit, and went into the kitchen, reappearing with a tureen of steaming soup.

"Emily will be along tomorrow," she said, as she served the soup; it had chunks of chicken and carrot floating in it. "She is rehearsing at nine, but told me she'll pay a visit in the afternoon. Now, eat." Telma pushed the fried bananas forward. "You like platano? Venga! You'll need the energy after coming all this way."

Carol did her best, but found the soup terribly salty and hard to swallow. The platanos were nice—though not very sweet. She nibbled at them and took small mouthfuls of the rice, which was sticky and came away in lumps on her spoon.

"Más! Come más!" said Telma, as Carol came to a halt.

"Oh, thank you, it's very nice, but I'm awfully tired. I don't think I can eat another mouthful."

"I made it for you *especially*." Telma's gaze was steady, but Carol, who could think only of closing her eyes against the darkness and sinking into sleep, stuck to her guns.

"As you wish," said the old lady finally with a shrug.

Carol woke early the next day to a tropical dawn; the light was reddish, not yet bright, and birds sang loudly. She lay for a while and listened. There was a dog barking, the sound of water on tin, and all around, the chatter of unfamiliar Cuban Spanish.

As she came down the stairs, she felt the morning air through the casement window, and the touch of ferns in the hallway on her legs, like silk. The dining table, already set for breakfast, held a dusky orange fruit she had never seen before, cut into chunks in a bowl. Next to it sat her muesli, a bunch of bananas and three very greasy eggs laid out on a plate.

"I've made you a cafecito." Telma pressed a tiny cup of black coffee into her hand. It was very sweet. "I've made you up some milk, as well." She offered a jug of watery white liquid. Carol poured it over the muesli, took a mouthful and gagged; it had a horrid taste—something she couldn't place, sour and ugly. She would have to find fresh milk as soon as possible—there must be somewhere you could get it here.

Telma pulled up a chair and sat opposite Carol while

she ate. Carol thought she should have asked first, but paid attention politely as the old lady talked.

"Do you like the fruit?" Telma was saying. "It's Emily's favourite—she says you don't have that one back home. We call it fruta bomba."

"Yes, it's very good."

"And how is it you know Emily?"

"I don't know her, really—she's the friend of a friend…"

Telma leaned in.

"He gave me her number—said she could help me find a place to stay."

"Oh yes, Emily is very kind, always helping others. She'll do anything for me. Are you a dancer too?"

"No, a teacher."

"One of the best professions."

Telma's hair was drawn into a kerchief but wisps of red escaped to frame her sallow face.

"My boss agreed to let me go for six months. It's called a sabbatical"—Carol said the word in English—"which basically means you take some time off and do what you want for a while."

"What luck." Telma sniffed.

"I know—I turned 35 this year, and I thought: it's now or never, I have to take the plunge."

Telma looked sad. "All my life… it's too late now… but I always wanted to go abroad when I was young. And then after the Revolución, of course, it was no longer possible. We don't have the same freedoms here that you do."

"We may have more *things* than you do, but that doesn't mean we're free," said Carol. "Some say we're slaves to money."

Telma swiped hard at a fly perched on the fruit. "But why Cuba?" she said. "What could we have to offer *you*?"

"Well, I'm travelling the whole of Latin America, but Cuba's my dream. You still have community here... compassion."

Telma rolled her eyes.

Carol took a last mouthful of fruit and gathered up her plates. Perhaps her Spanish wasn't good enough yet to discuss these things.

"No, let me do that," said Telma. "You go and look around outside before it gets too hot."

Carol went to her room. It was only 10 o'clock, but the sun already beat against the skylight. She rummaged through her suitcase for a hat, and rubbed factor-30 lotion into her skin. Tropical sun was cruel, she knew.

Outside, the air smelled of summer mixed with burning gasoline. Birds sang noisily, forgetting they were in the middle of a city, and flowers burst from cracks in the pavement, clamouring for the sun. There was no nook or cranny without some green luscious thing. It was too hot for more than a slow stroll, and besides, there seemed to be so much time. People stood about talking, or sat outside their houses, soaking up the day. Children ran free, not a parent in sight, and from behind an iron gate she caught a glimpse of people dancing, clapping to a rhythmic, insistent drumming, and standing in a ring.

At the bottom of the avenue, where old Spanish-style houses gave way to ugly prefab blocks, she came to a main road; directly beyond it was the sea, burnished blue and quivering beneath the sun. There was no one in sight apart from a man sitting on the coast wall fishing with a piece of string, a plastic spider for bait. Moments later another man appeared, snorkelling up from under the waves—blue fins surfacing first, then the rest of him, tumbled by the swirl onto spiky rocks where crabs lay basking in the warmth. The man jumped out of the water, and Carol saw that he was holding a ring with fish hooked onto it. They kept trying to flip back into the sea but before they could escape, the man took a knife to them and scraped away their scales.

Later that afternoon, Carol was woken from a nap by a cheerful "Hello!" and a head of blond hair around her bedroom door. It was Emily—younger and prettier than Carol had imagined on the phone.

"How's it going?" Emily said. "I thought I'd let you settle in before coming over to show you stuff."

"Oh fine, thanks. I'm… adjusting."

"Yeah, it's pretty different. I remember when I arrived—I stayed here with Telma, and I thought: oh my God, what am I doing? But you soon settle in and make friends, and then it's just like normal life."

"Telma's taking care of me. I really appreciate your helping me find a place to stay."

"No problem. Telma's great. Really kind, but a bit old school. She's nearly 70—you've got to respect her ways." Emily sat down on the bed.

"Where are you living now?"

"In a student room at the dance school. Listen, I thought we'd do a tour of the barrio—help you find your feet."

On the way out, Telma pinched Emily's cheeks and forced a sweet cake down her throat as if she were a little bird. Emily kissed her, exclaiming, "Mamita! You always take care of me!"

They stepped out into the sun, past a couple sitting arm-in-arm on the porch. "Be careful with the neighbours," Emily said. "Just don't be too friendly, 'cos Telma's room isn't legal—she doesn't pay the licence fee so officially she's not allowed to rent it out. If she gets caught with you here she'll pay a thousand-dollar fine. So—careful who you talk to when you come and go."

"Would the neighbours tell?"

"Well, most not. But you never know. There's someone on every block who keeps an eye on things, and if they find out — well…"

They walked to the dollar store, where Emily said Carol could buy things like milk, tuna and imported cheese, and then to a hotel, where she could send and receive faxes. Along the coast wall, which was called the Malecón, there was a market with people queuing to buy pumpkins, pineapples and bananas. The market was in pesos, Emily said — this was what the Cubans earned, but anything worth buying was sold at the dollar store; peso shops were often empty or sold shabby, inferior goods.

As they climbed the avenue towards the house, they passed two men sitting on a wall who blew them kisses and made a hissing sound. Carol stiffened and stared straight ahead, but Emily called something back in Spanish, which made the men laugh. To Carol she said: "I used to think it was incredibly sexist, all that stuff, but I don't mind it now, in fact I like it — it makes me feel more of a woman."

Carol nodded. She wasn't sure she'd get used to that kind of attention, but life was certainly opening up.

Carol spent the next few days exploring Havana. She enrolled in an advanced Spanish course at the university; this took up her mornings, leaving afternoons free for the sights. As the days went on, she found herself on the receiving end of far more attention than she had bargained for — even though she did everything possible to avoid standing out. She wore dresses and shoes, rather than the tourist uniform of shorts and sandals, never carried a water bottle, and moved about slowly instead of hurrying from place to place. But there was something in the Cuban women she simply couldn't match — they were haughty, walking with nonchalance, oblivious to the whistles and stares. Cubanas kept their men at bay, while Carol's pale, slightly anxious face drew them in like flies.

About a week after Carol's arrival, Telma announced that her grandson, Raúl, would be joining them that night. Raúl lived in the building next door—he'd been away in Matanzas with a cousin. The prospect pleased Carol. Emily had not visited since the day of their barrio tour, and she was starting to feel a little bored. Her fellow students were all much younger than she was, and would go off together after class—where, she had no idea. While Telma could always be relied upon for company in the evenings, Carol had begun to yearn for friendship with someone closer to her age.

Raúl's arrival was announced by a scattered tapping knock. He had an odd pageboy haircut and reddish, freckled skin showing from underneath a US baseball vest. His voice was strange: it had a rather petulant tone, hovering for ages on a single vowel before descending to a shallow base note, then rising again.

Telma served them coffee and settled down to watch TV.

Carol was pleased to discover that Raúl spoke almost perfect English. He told her that he used to be an engineer but, at 29, got fed up with working for the state wage of $18 a month and gave it up to conduct a little "business" of his own. Now he lived from an illegal internet connection rigged up to Telma's phone, sending emails for 50 cents apiece. He took Carol out to the back and showed her the line he'd strung from his apartment to Telma's, connecting his computer to her phone—Cubans weren't allowed the internet at home.

They were interrupted by Telma.

"Fidel, Fidel, Fidel!" she mouthed contemptuously, waving one wrinkled arm at the television, her face twisted with anger. The president was giving his nightly speech. Raúl moved smartly over to the set and switched it to the other channel, where some children in leotards were dancing to a disco tune. He laughed sheepishly at Carol.

"You can see we're not supporters of the Revolution in this house," he said. "Telma cried the day it began." He laughed again and moved back to where they had been sitting at the table, as if nothing had happened.

Carol wanted to ask why they didn't support the Revolution. She'd read that Cuba had a higher literacy rate than anywhere in Latin America, and free healthcare for all; that the Revolution had done away with a terrible inequality between the working classes and the bourgeoisie. But before she could say anything, Telma spoke again: "He has robbed us! This country—ruined!"—her voice quavered—"Before he came we were rich, and now we have nothing, we *are* nothing… Poor! We live like rats!" She gestured around the room, which was, by Western standards, humbly furnished. But that was part of its charm. It wasn't dirty and the walls were nicely painted—much better than some of the wrecks Carol had seen along the street.

"That man has stolen our lives. If I were younger I'd leave on one of the boats like your mother did," Telma said. "And now he's taking *you*… My Raúl, the only thing I have left."

"Shh, Grandma, shh. I'm not going yet." He put an arm round her shoulders. Carol remained at the table, fiddling with her cup of coffee. After a moment, Raúl looked over to Carol and smiled. "Don't worry. Telma can get a little upset. She knows that I want to leave, but soon she forgets." To Telma he said: "Now, come on. Let's sit down together and speak of happy things, OK?"

At 11 o'clock Raúl said he had to go. He kissed Carol on the cheek and gave her a knowing look. "Telma worries too much, just ignore it—she can be a little fuerte." As he left, he added: "Remember, I'm at your service. Anything you need—I'm here to help."

"Yes. My Raúl will look after you," Telma said, turning her face up to him as he bent to kiss her goodbye.

On Wednesday the following week, as Carol was finishing her morning coffee, the telephone rang. It was Emily. Telma's face lit up as she held the receiver to her ear: "Mami!" she said. "Good to hear from you—you've been a stranger! Yes, Carol is well… you want to talk with her?" She handed Carol the phone.

"Carol, how are you? What have you been up to—having fun?" Emily's voice was warm and clear. "Listen, I was thinking, do you want to meet up later? I can show you round Old Havana if you like."

They agreed to meet at two o'clock at the top of Calle Obispo, which led to Old Havana. Carol was already waiting when Emily jumped out of a little black Lada that screeched round the corner, almost knocking down a man at the kerb. Emily thrust a dollar bill into the driver's hand and they moved off down the narrow, crowded street.

Past half-empty peso shops, and vast stretches of dug-up road where dust filled the air, they came to a quiet cobbled square whose old colonial houses had been repainted and restored. Only one or two still leaned precariously into scaffolds—people lived in them, evidently, from the washing strung across the balconies, but Emily said they'd soon be moved out and restoration complete. This was Old Havana, ready for the tourist trade.

As they walked through an archway to a promenade beside the sea, Carol drew in her breath; stretching off into the distance were hundreds of coloured canvasses—artists selling their work. Carol knew straight away that she would buy a painting; it would make the room at Telma's really hers. The colours were bright—turquoise, scarlet, gold—and the styles abstract like Picasso, or fantastic like Chagall. After a couple of minutes she found a canvas that clearly represented Havana, with rows of houses stacked on a hill curving round a bay. She bought it for $20 and the stall-owner wrapped it in brown paper.

"Great choice," said Emily. "Is that for your room?"

"Yes, to make it feel like home."

"How are you getting on at Telma's then?"

"Good—they treat me like family. And Raúl's really nice."

Emily smiled. "Yeah, they've been like that for me too."

"You know, Emily, I was afraid I'd be lonely when I came—but I haven't felt alone for a second. There's always someone to talk to. It's so warm, so different from London."

"I totally know what you mean. People here live in such a close way it's impossible to be alone—even if you just have a chat with the vegetable man at the bottom of the street."

"When I came here," said Carol carefully, not wanting to appear too strange, "I… knew I was looking for something, though I wasn't sure what exactly. Life back home seemed… shallow… People in London don't have time for anything except themselves—or their careers. It's just so empty, work a 10-hour day then go out and get drunk. I knew there must be more…"

They had stopped in front of a peso shop and were staring into a window of fake gold jewellery and dusty cups. Carol waited for Emily's response, wondering if she'd said too much, but Emily seemed to have lost interest—she wandered into the shop and began an animated conversation with the three men who stood behind the counter.

Carol crossed the street to a woman who stood by an array of plastic flowers laid out on a rickety table. A sign said: *Three pesos each.* She picked a red rose for Telma, and the woman smiled at her through a mouthful of missing teeth. "Mi amor, I'll make it pretty for you. Be kind and give me a dollar will you please?" Carol took the flower, which the woman had decorated with a piece of shiny yellow ribbon, and handed over three pesos. She decided against the dollar, though. If her funds were to last the trip there could be no unnecessary spending, no matter how small. The woman thanked her with a gracious nod and Carol went to join Emily, who was standing outside the shop.

Telma was delighted with the rose. She added it with great ceremony to her plastic flower collection in a vase by the TV, and planted a dry kiss on Carol's cheek. "You are like a daughter to me," she said, clasping Carol's hand in her bony fingers. "Here, my dear, take this." She unwound the yellow ribbon from the rose and gave it to Carol. "Now, you'll want to wash before dinner, won't you? I've made you fried chicken—cheap in the market today, fifteen pesos the pound."

Upstairs, Carol put the painting of Havana on the shelf above her bed. It looked nice there. Her books had been cleared away and the shelf dusted clean. After some thought, she tied the yellow ribbon around a corner of the mirror by the door.

As Carol ate her dinner, a restlessness started creeping in. Havana seemed to be full of clubs and bars, but it would be asking for trouble to wander out alone. The one night she'd gone to get an ice-cream, two men had tailed her, sharp in suits and shiny shoes, insisting they could show her round.

"So, are you off out tonight?" asked Telma.

"Oh, no," said Carol. "No. I think I'll stay and talk to you." The old lady raised her eyebrows but did not look away from the TV. "I like it," Carol found herself saying. "It's peaceful here. So different from the rush of home." She added an insouciant laugh to prevent any further questioning.

Telma ignored this.

"A young person like you should be out having fun, not sitting at home with me," she said. "Raúl must take you dancing."

When Raúl arrived for dinner, Telma spoke to him rapidly in Spanish, gesturing in Carol's direction. Carol felt embarrassed, but then Raúl came over looking slightly apologetic, which made things better, and said: "Grandma says I ought to take you out. What do you think? She's quite insistent." He rolled his eyes comically behind Telma's back and Carol laughed.

"If you put it that way—your grandma's very kind to think of me."

"So, get ready. I'll come for you at ten."

They were to go to Casa de la Amistad, a little club nearby whose music often drifted over the rooftops to Carol's room at night. In some excitement, she put on a flowery silk dress she'd bought just before leaving London, and a pair of strappy heels. Telma had painted her toenails for her—they glowed sugar-pink. Turning sideways in the mirror, she saw that she'd put on a little weight—but that didn't matter, women were allowed to have stomachs here.

At ten exactly Raúl arrived. "Beautiful!" he said with a wink when he saw Carol. He opened the door for her and steered her to the club with a gentle pressure to the shoulder. As they arrived, he stepped back, allowing her to pay. It cost $5—roughly twenty times the price of a night out in a peso bar, he said. They walked through to a lush garden at the back where there were tables, and a salsa band playing on a stage. Raúl pulled out Carol's chair for her and refused a drink, until, at Carol's insistence, he ordered a cola, opening it only once her beer had arrived and he'd poured it into the glass.

"You dance?" he said.

"Well, not really... But I'd like to try."

"May I?" He held out his hand and led her to the floor. "Relax, listen to the beat and follow me."

He took her in his arms and they began to dance, Carol slightly hesitant at first and then getting it as he led her deftly in time. Every now and then he'd put a hand on her hips, moving them back and forth, and say: "You see—like that." After a couple of tunes they sat down, pleased, to watch the other dancers. Carol hoped she didn't look as bad as them. They were mostly Europeans, and had no movement at all in their hips, just jiggled their upper bodies in a hopeless attempt at keeping time.

Raúl wanted to know all about her life in England: how much apartments cost, how much she earned, and whether people were given houses by the government after marriage or had to stay at home with their parents. Carol did her best to fill him in, but it was a bit like talking to a man from another planet—even the basics had to be explained. After listening for a while, Raúl fell into a gloomy mood.

"There is no future for us here," he said. "You cannot know how hard it is."

"But what is so bad about here? I really don't see—you've got a place to live, food, education, and many things that we don't have back home."

"Maybe to you it seems that way, but you don't know really what our life is like. You come here, I understand, because you believe we're a nation of happy people. You see us making music, laughing at our troubles. You dance. But what do you really see? Not our struggle, not our sadness."

"But Raúl, honestly, in our society there's poverty too—terrible poverty, and crime. And riches for a few. At least here you're all equal and you care for each other. Socialism may seem hard to you, but capitalism is far more cruel."

"Please, don't talk to me about socialism. It is something you cannot possibly understand. You have not lived it. Stick to talking about what you know." Raúl pursed his lips so hard that they became thin and white, and he fell silent.

Carol was angry. If he disagreed with her views, then he was free to say so and they could argue it out. This childish silence really was a pain. But feeling the awkwardness growing between them, she decided to call a truce. "OK, sorry. Let's talk about something else."

They sat for a while longer under the clear night; they did not dance again. Raúl refused another drink and seemed lost in thought. He was pleasant enough, though, and when the time came to go home, he steered Carol to Telma's door with the same courtesy as he had shown before.

She woke the next morning to the sound of the dog barking insanely then suddenly silent as if someone had shot it. A neighbour was on his balcony, bellowing to family members inside; he seemed not to consider communicating at close range, but simply shouted as loud as possible so that whomever he was addressing might hear. Telma was clattering about in the kitchen beneath, and someone hammered relentlessly on stone. Carol sighed and sat up. Clearly there was to be no peace, so she might as well begin her day.

She sprinted downstairs and snatched a plate of fruta bomba from the old fridge in the corridor, running back up quickly so Telma couldn't collar her and ask about the night before. She would, she decided, skip school today and brave the streets to make the trip to the National Museum of Fine Arts that she had been promising herself since she'd arrived.

"Your breakfast isn't ready yet," said Telma, when Carol descended, dressed and ready to go. "Aren't you stopping for something to eat?" The floor was all wet from where she had been mopping.

"No—I'll get something on the way."

"Where are you going? It's far too early for school... Be careful of that food they sell on the street. Your insides aren't tough like ours, you know—used to all sorts of things."

"Telma, please don't fuss. I'll be back for my dinner at seven." And with that, she left, ignoring the curious looks from the neighbours who sat on the step. Emily's warning had sunk in—and besides, they never seemed especially friendly.

Of all the hot and humid days so far, this one seemed particularly fierce. The ground shivered and belted back the heat. Within two minutes of leaving the building, Carol's freshly washed body was running in sweat. She'd spent all her dollars and the bank didn't open until 10 o'clock. Unsure of how to hail a peso taxi, and certain she couldn't find her way by bus, she decided to walk, using the street map in the Cuba book as her guide.

She made her way along Calle 23, past the university and down into Central Havana. The streets here were dirtier than those where Telma lived; piles of rubbish festered in the gullies, covered with flies, and she almost stepped on a dead rat that lay sprawled across the pavement. The shop windows were empty, apart from a few pencils laid out on a yellow card, or faded, dusty shirts on wire coat hangers that appeared to have been manufactured some time in the '70s. Ancient, rotating fans built into the sides of buildings lay silent and people walked under the shelter of umbrellas or sat quietly in the shade, but Carol pounded on.

She came to a halt in front of a window that displayed an old dry bun on a stool next to a sign that said: *Pasta con carne y jugo de mango*. It was a cafetería. Inside, at the tiniest of wire tables, people were eating buns. Carol's stomach crawled with hunger but before she could make up her mind whether it would be wise to enter, she was distracted by two boys shouting: "Hey, lady! Where you from?" — "Want to rent a room?"

She ignored them and walked off, staring straight ahead, but the boys tailed her. She moved sideways, they did too; she slowed down, they held back.

"Lady, lady! Spik Ingleesh? *Francés*?"

She turned off the street and walked in a determined fashion for a few minutes before coming to a dead end, nothing but a tall apartment building and a yawning door ahead. The boys had stopped a few feet away and were giggling, waiting to see what she would do next.

A woman sat on a chair in the doorway, staring at Carol, and from outside other houses nearby, several pairs of eyes gazed, unhurried, slow. No one came forward or offered to help; they simply waited and watched. Carol shrank away.

"The way to the National Museum of Fine Arts, please?" she said finally to the woman on the chair. The woman shrugged and pointed towards the streets she had come from. The boys tittered; everyone else kept up the silent stares. Carol hurried off back the way she'd come, almost running, and reached a maze of smaller streets. She took one at random and walked rapidly until she was sure the boys had gone. Round a corner, she came to a steep, wide hill, almost empty of cars, and saw the Malecón at its end; a crowd of people with rucksacks, dressed in shorts and sandals, hovered by the wall. She slipped gratefully among them.

A few days later, she was at the table waiting for her dinner when Telma bore in a plate of greying tuna garnished with raw onion rings. Carol was sure the tuna was from a tin that she had located in the dollar shop one day.

"Telma," she said. "That tuna was mine—I was going to use it to make sandwiches for my lunch."

Telma paused, setting the fish down carefully on the table between the soup and the rice, gathering herself, like a balloon filling with air.

"Well, I'm sure, if you don't want me touching your things, you only have to say."

"No, it's not that—it's just that the tuna took me ages to find and I wish you'd asked me first."

Telma banged down a glass of water with unnecessary force. "Oh! If we're dividing up what's yours and mine, then please do forgive me if I touched something that is *yours*."

"Look, there's no need to be like that. I'd just prefer it if you asked before you took my things."

Telma's eyes screwed into little purple points. "I share all my things with you—and you take what you want!"

"No, I don't. I never take anything of yours without asking first."

"I hadn't realised there was such a separation. I treat you like my *family*."

"Yes, but I'm *not* your family, I'm your… *lodger*… I pay you twelve dollars a day for my bed and… meals." Carol was struggling to get the Spanish words out and found the pitch of her voice rising to compensate.

"Ay, mi madre! From now on, you can go to the market and buy the food yourself. Cook your own meals. Here, I'll put the tuna back in the fridge so you can have it for your lunch." Telma swept the plate off the table.

"Please, Telma. It's difficult—I can't say things exactly how I mean them in Spanish—"

"—Oh, your Spanish is very good. You know perfectly well what you're saying."

"I don't! You don't understand!" Carol felt her eyes pricking, and she stood up to make her point. "It's not fair, you are deliberately misunderstanding what I say." She waved an arm in Telma's direction for emphasis.

"Oh, I think I understand very well." Telma's face was like a shut gate. "Please do not shout. I am not your servant." She went into the kitchen, leaving Carol standing there beside her empty plate. Moments later she returned to serve the meal, but Carol found she could not eat. She rose and made her way to her room.

When she woke the next morning the sun was already high. Voices floated up the stairs—mainly Telma's, and every now and then a syllable or two from Raúl.

Raúl would help, Carol thought. She would explain to him in English what had happened and everything would be all right. Last night things had got out of control and Telma had taken it all the wrong way. Raúl was her friend, he would understand.

She pulled on her robe and splashed some water over her face. When she was sure that the talking had stopped, she went downstairs to the kitchen where Telma was scrubbing vigorously at some dishes. The old lady did not look up, but said "Buenos días" as if nothing had happened. Raúl had gone. Carol drank her coffee on the balcony, then dressed and slipped next door. Raúl was out, but would be back by three, his neighbour said, letting Carol in to leave a note. *Please come and see me—I need to talk to you*, she wrote on a slip of paper, and placed it on the computer keyboard where Raúl would be sure to see it right away.

Carol sat in her room and tried to read. All she could think of was the night before. She wanted to phone home, but all the international operators were busy and you couldn't call direct. Waiting was hard, but she had to wait—until things were put right she couldn't face going downstairs.

Raúl didn't come till evening. At eight o'clock she heard his familiar knock, then footsteps as he climbed the staircase to her room, tapping briskly on her door. Carol took a deep breath and prepared to unburden herself. Everything would be all right now, justified and explained.

Raúl did not greet her in his usual friendly way, but simply pulled a chair round and sat astride it, leaning his forearms on the back.

"Right. So?" His face looked red and puffy, his brown eyes slightly opaque. She noticed that his shoulder-length bob was cut in a perfectly straight line.

"I know that Telma's been talking about me, and I just want you to hear my side of the story," Carol began, looking for some sign of encouragement.

"She said you shouted at her and told her not to touch your food."

"Well, no, not exactly. I certainly didn't shout."

"She said you did."

Carol frowned. "Maybe she misunderstood—my Spanish

isn't the best, especially in the middle of an argument."

"So what exactly *did* you say?"

"I said I needed the tuna for lunch, and I'd prefer it if she asked me before using my things."

"That's not what she told me. I know Telma—I know she wouldn't lie."

"But Raúl, can't you see she might lie because she feels ashamed?"

"Why should she feel ashamed?"

"Because she's been unfair. I was asking a perfectly reasonable thing, and she didn't like it—she wants everything her own way. And now she's turning it all around because I'm the stranger—I'm the one you won't believe."

Raúl looked doubtful. She took the opportunity to push her point home: "Look, try to imagine you're a foreigner in someone else's house, you know no one and can't speak the language very well. Imagine how vulnerable you'd be."

"I don't think you're vulnerable at all," he said. "You're getting a very good deal. Where else in this city would you get meals and a bed for twelve dollars a night?"

"That's not the point! It's only cheap because Telma doesn't pay the licence fee—she'd charge far more if she did." Carol's voice wavered. "You said we were friends… you were here to *help*, you said."

"You misunderstand me. To help, yes. But friendship? I hardly know you."

"Please believe me," Carol said. "I'm in your home, your family… believe me… I am telling the truth."

"No," said Raúl. "I don't believe you. I think you are a liar." With that, he rose and left the room.

Carol lay on the bed. She stared at the counterpane for a long time; its frayed cotton lines looked like waves across the sea. As night deepened and quiet fell, she heard simply the click of the fan in the darkness and the rhythm of her heart.

Early the following morning the telephone rang. No one was answering; the old lady must be out. Carol picked up the receiver—it was Emily.

"What's up?" Emily said. "Telma says you've had a row."

"Emily, I didn't shout at her—she just didn't understand."

"Hey, slow down. What happened?"

"I tried to tell Raúl, but he won't listen—he thinks I'm a liar."

Emily was quiet for a moment, then she said: "Look, come and meet me for a coffee. I've got some time before class. We can talk."

Carol walked two blocks to the cafetería on Calle 23. The city was boiling, a blister about to burst. Emily was already waiting when Carol arrived, her dance kit in a bag beside her, reading; she looked up with concern, but her expression was not unkind. Carol ordered a coffee and told Emily about the argument, trembling slightly when she came to the part about Raúl. When she had finished there was silence as Emily sat and thought, chewing things over.

"I spoke to Telma about it," she said slowly. "And she is very upset. I know that Telma can be emotional… exaggerate. But I can't imagine she'd *lie.*"

Carol felt something inside her falling. "Why doesn't anyone believe me? What do I have to do to make you see that I'm telling the truth?"

"Carol… it's just that we know Telma so well. It's hard to believe she'd want to hurt you, and to be honest, I've only just met you… I mean, I've tried to be a friend while you're here but it's up to you to win people's respect."

Carol gazed at the table top.

"The closeness here works both ways—you're known and loved, but being known like that means you can't hide."

Carol finished her coffee and thanked Emily for her time. Then she walked to Infanta and hailed a taxi to the Air France office. The woman behind the desk told Carol that the next flight to Mexico City departed in two days' time; she could book into Hotel Inglaterra — there were rooms available — at $100 a night.

The apartment was quiet when Carol returned; nothing was cooking on the stove and Telma was out. She took down the painting of Havana and left it outside at the back by the bins, then she packed her suitcases and swept out the cupboards and under the bed. When she was sure that everything was as it had been on her arrival and not a trace of her remained, she sat down on the bed and drank a glass of water. It was three o'clock.

Before dragging her suitcases down the stairs, Carol took a last look around the room. She walked over to the mirror and removed the twist of yellow ribbon, throwing it into the wastepaper basket as she left.

THE PARTY

SUNDAY MORNING. WE took a peso taxi to the Capitolio and then another to Alamar—a big red car with red leather seats and a courting couple in the front, him pecking her ear. Out of Centro Havana we drove, through dusty, broken suburbs where the air smelled of plastic and ships rotted in the sea. Soon there were no pretty buildings, just breeze-block flats, endless pink and grey boxes squatting in the scrubby bush.

My feet were dirty. I was wearing my favourite burgundy dress with white sandals, toes painted gold. I pushed my foot against his.

"That is... impolite?" He giggled.

"So you *were* studying yesterday."

He wrapped me closer. "I lob you." We bit the corners of each others' lips and swigged from a bottle of rum. We'd been together all yesterday in our room in Havana—he wrapped in the chenille bedspread, studying from the red English book I'd given him, me too lazy to finish the letter I'd begun to my mother—together on the big bed, his clear eyes inches away. He treasured the shiny red English book, better than anything. Just like the pound coin—he'd pulled it from his wallet the day I arrived and kissed it to his lips.

We got out on a corner and paid 20 pesos. At the end of the street stood a disused warehouse in its own plot. The ground floor was empty, but upstairs, round to the side, was Ramón's. Charro straightened up and moved, faster than usual, towards the house. I pulled at his shirt. Just one more time—I wanted to hear it before we got on our best behaviour with his family. "Your English is getting pretty good. Say it again—what you said in the car."

"I lob you, honey."

Ramón and his woman, Mirna, stood at the top of the steps staring, as if they did not know how to speak.

"Qué bolá?" said Charro, hugging Ramón, who was much smaller than him. "This is Anna."

"Mucho gusto." I clung to Charro's bicep.

"Ven, ven." Mirna pulled me by the hand.

The place seemed empty apart from a matte silver TV in one corner, but as my sun-blind eyes adjusted I noticed a threadbare sofa and a red plastic rocking chair. A fan blew wildly from side to side.

"Sit," said Charro, nudging me onto the sofa.

"Sit, Anna," said Mirna.

There was a gust of wind; spits of rain came through the shutters. Charro closed them and brushed the drops from my neck with his fingertips.

They clustered into another room behind a curtain at the back. I tried to hear what they were saying but it was hard to make much out. There was a single orange flower displayed upon a shelf and an old woman was cooking in a dirty kitchenette off to the side. I felt thirsty, but they were laughing and I couldn't remember the polite way to ask for a drink.

So many flies—in the city there weren't this many. I felt an emptiness in the pit of my stomach and thought that touching Charro would stop it, would anchor me at least to our room in Havana, the place where I knew him and he knew me. I had to get a drink. I would talk to the old woman, she would help.

"I'm Anna." I held out my hand. She carried on pounding something in a smashed-up pan. "How are you?"

"Regular." The woman leaned against the counter and rubbed the base of her neck. "Sometimes I get an attack of the nerves… It's normal at my age."

Her glasses were held together with tape. "I have these." She lifted up her dress and pointed to her thighs. The skin was all bumpy.

"How old are you?"

"Seventy!"

A baby waddled in, naked but for a pair of flapping, flannel shorts.

"Here, Anna." Mirna placed a glass in front of me. "Charro says that you like tea."

"Muchas gracias." I took the glass. Sweet and brown, but not tea.

I wanted Charro, but it was Mirna who sat beside me in the rocker, breastfeeding the baby.

"What's his name?" I touched the baby's head.

"Frankie."

His squinty eyes did not respond.

"Precioso," I said.

A dog wandered through a side door and sniffed my feet.

"Where has Charro gone?"

"Men… out on the street… who knows?" Mirna shrugged.

The old woman stayed in the kitchenette and cooked.

Cracked brown shutters kept out the sun but when the rain fell the sound was not as good as glass.

The guests began to arrive at Noon. There was fat mulatta Barbara and her husband Ivan, who was small and stocky with a broken right arm. I sat between them on the sofa.

"Cuántos años...?" I began.

"I married him at 17," Barbara said.

Gretchen, their doe-eyed daughter, was bigger than she was. The girl sat with her arms around her mother.

"Now, Caridad," said Barbara, glancing over to a square, solid woman with scraped-back hair who was perched on the sofa arm, "You don't take any shit, do you Caridad?" — to me — "*She* is divorced two times."

The woman nodded but kept her mouth shut.

"Me," Barbara lifted her eyes in praise, "I have my daughter."

"Fatty!" Gretchen pinched Barbara's midriff and Barbara, bursting from striped trousers and a gold-button blouse, looked down and laughed.

"You must always be true to yourself." My words split the warm round speech around me. I was nodding and trying to look into their eyes, imagining it like a group of girlfriends from home, where I would talk empathetically about man problems and the need to be strong, but what I wanted was Charro.

"We got it, Caridad..." Barbara turned from Caridad and spoke to me in a stage whisper. "Ivan — he managed to get the permit, for the house." She made a duck-like movement with one palm.

"But..." I said, "How, if... I thought that foreigners were the only ones who got the building — ?"

" — in Cuba, amor, you have to understand, he says one thing, he does another. In Cuba, we have a *doble moral*. We are smiling on our face, like this…" she made a bright, fake smile at an imaginary person off to the side, "and we are doing, how do you say? Under… under…"

"The counter?"

"The counter. Under it, we are doing *this*." She pretended to slip something round the back of the sofa arm. The music of Cuban Spanish was different to mine; it sounded as if everything was said tongue-in-cheek.

"You and Charro." Barbara winked.

"… if I could find him."

"Take him—take him from here." Her voice became low and urgent. "To England. You must do that. I don't know what it is you have to do exactly, but you have to make some papers. It is terrible living here. You *must*." She gripped my hand in both of hers.

The music playing was a loud, discordant salsa. Even though the bass had been turned right up, the treble squealed through the air. I caught sight of a man in the corner of the room; his nose was dripping and he wiped it on a folded handkerchief, a white one. He saw me looking and stared back.

"That's Jorge," said Barbara. "You like? Be careful."

Soon Ivan's green eyes began to glaze over with the rum and he fell to quarrelling with Barbara—she petulant, he shouting louder and louder to hold her attention. Wedged between them, I looked for Charro and now I saw him. He was in the kitchenette. Why hadn't I seen him come in? And why hadn't he said hello? I rushed over and grabbed him round the waist. He was making fan patterns on the edge of pasties with a fork.

"Sweetheart." I nudged his shoulder with my chin.

"Honey, move." His right arm was trapped.

"Sit with me."

"I'm doing this."

"Don't leave me alone," I said into his ear.

"You're not alone—talk to Mirna. Dance."

I pouted. "Who with?"

His back was rigid, muscled from hauling, lifting, chopping. Sometimes, though, he was fluid, when music was playing—like a marionette without its strings.

"Change your face." He carried on making imprints in the dough. It surprised me that he could do such small movements so well. Then he pointed with his eyes to the old woman, who was cooking next to him. She was Mirna's mother or aunt. All morning she had been slicing, boiling and washing. She wiped cracked blue tiles clean of food and began again; plates piled up—dirty plates with bits of food and forks—and she washed them; she took the baby when he cried, her eyes just visible from behind her glasses, barely there. She probably needed his help.

Out in the salón, the women were holding little Frankie, his eyes round and unsmiling, waving his arms for him in time to the music. "Baila! Baila!" they chanted. He looked bewildered, clutched onto the side of a chair, and when no one was watching any more, waggled his bottom in time to the beat.

I danced with Ramón on the balcony. Much smaller, Ramón made me stoop to meet his rhythm and the guests crowded round, fascinated, like spectators at a dogfight. Ivan was gesturing at Jorge—they laughed and shouted to each other, *She knows how to dance!* They stood around us in a ring; Ivan's eyes seemed to bulge larger and larger in his small head until I thought they might burst from their sockets. "Mira cómo le gusta mover el culo!" he cried, slapping his thigh.

Then it was Mirna with Ramón. She moved vaguely in yellow shorts. I stood to one side. A smile turned the corners of her mouth but it was not at Ramón that she threw her gaze.

"Here he is," said Barbara. "The other half of your… How you say? The other piece of your… Orange?"

Charro caught my wrist and we danced. At first he held me tentatively, as if I might break, or as if I was really strong and might hurt him. I focused hard on my feet—one two three, one two three—on the steps he'd taught.

"Amor, look at me." He lifted my face to his, cradled me, swung me round till my feet, which knew the steps, no longer knew but moved of their own accord; turned me with the slightest pressure, the flick of a wrist.

"*That's* it." He held me tight, as if there'd been no time in between, and we kissed. There were no words that needed to be said that might not be said, no painful silences. It was just us in the heartbeat of the dance.

The old woman was leaning against the counter, staring at us with a peculiar look in her eyes—almost as if she was angry, remembering a time when she would have been the one dancing, thinking of romance long gone, and she alone, left to cook in a dirty kitchen. I saw my mother, youth etched beneath her sagging face; I saw the future with her not there.

"What will happen when I'm old?" I whispered to Charro.

"Come to Cuba."

"Will you look after me?"

"Of course." His breath was sweet with rum.

Jorge grabbed me out of Charro's arms. Charro stumbled backwards then regained his balance. Jorge motioned towards Charro, two fingers crushed together. "I need a girlfriend." He leered at me, swaying slightly. "But all the women in Havana are locas."

Charro's face was still. He stood; courteous, upright.

Jorge had me clamped in his meaty arms. He stamped out of time. "Dance!" His eyes were bloodshot. "Hasn't your

Cubano taught you how? Come on!"

I stumbled, as if my bones had become disconnected.

"Dance, honey!" Charro began to laugh. I was so clumsy. They were all laughing and smiling around us. "Move it, chica!" shouted Barbara. Why couldn't anyone see that Jorge was revolting—that this was revolting? Only Caridad hung back, grim-faced on the sofa.

"No!" I pulled my hand out of Jorge's. "*Charro* is my boyfriend. Don't!"

I rushed to the side of the room. Charro didn't follow, he just continued tapping in time to the salsa, then pulled Mirna into a dance. I kept on looking at him, but he wouldn't meet my eye. The sweat on my back felt cold.

After the dancing it got chilly and we were hungry. Charro and the men went to buy oil; I refused to give them five dollars for it. They drove off in a truck and I sat on the balcony staring and staring with the others down at other people staring back at us from the street. The only life was in the children. A group of little girls, pretty twisted bows and curls, scattered like hundreds and thousands across the street. Boys played baseball without a bat, big shorts slung low, riding their skinny hips.

A girl whined to her mother. A glass fell and smashed.

The party seemed to have fallen into despair. Music still blared from the ghetto blaster but the guests had sunk into a torpor, staring listlessly into space. A man, big-boned and toothless, roused himself into a thumping, flailing dance. The others looked away.

"I went to the Soviet Union in 1993," Caridad was saying to me. We were sitting on the sofa, which had been dragged onto the balcony. "They had a wonderful life—I don't know why they changed. Wonderful. So many opportunities... They had everything."

"But... Wasn't it...?"—I clasped my hands—"I mean,

didn't a lot of Russians come *here*?"

She brushed a crumb from her skirt. "It was very hard here during the Special Period. We had nothing. No soap, no shampoo. Now is a little better, but the tourists are bad for Cuba." She pointed at her shoes; they were broken and her feet blistered and swollen. "Now all anybody wants is dollars. No one wants pesos any more, and you can only get four dollars for 100 pesos, which is what I earn at the market a month."

"… terrible …" I flushed. "So, you're getting married? That's nice."

"Next month. My third." She looked determined.

"Congratulations."

"I don't like to suffer."

"How do you know when it's time to leave?"

"When they betray me with another woman, or when the arguments begin. My second husband, he left for Miami in a speedboat, but I didn't want to go with him. This one is getting a Spanish passport because he had a Spanish grandfather and then we're going to Spain."

"When I'm in love, I can't leave even if they're shit." I meant to laugh but it came out as a yelp.

"Cuban women, we give our sex but not ourselves." She leaned in. Her eyes were ringed with bright blue kohl, the lashes crushed and knotted. "He only wants your money."

There were three tin pots at the edge of the balcony, next to a cement balustrade ringed with rusty barbed wire. A tattered pink towel hung from the washing line.

"Charro's not like that."

We sat on the sofa for a bit in the dark, with just a small neon light tacked up above the door.

When Charro returned he set to kneading dough in the kitchen. He fried chunks of ham with garlic and tomatoes, kneaded and kneaded the dry white dough on the cracked, blue china tiles.

I stood near and picked at one of the pasties.

"Yummy?" he asked.

"You don't like dancing with me."

"Honey." He flicked some oil into the hot pan.

"You don't think I'm as good as a Cuban woman. You don't like it when I dance. Do you prefer black women?"

He thought for a minute, pressing one finger onto his mouth. "Black… They are more amorosas." He bared the gold heart welded to his front tooth.

I turned away.

"On the inside you are black. Caliente like a cubana."

Mirna came into the kitchen. She lifted the lid off one of the aluminium pots. "Anna, don't eat too much—I want to make sure that you have some of this." She shuffled me so that my face was over the pot; steam hit my eyes. The pot contained a large bone with a shred of meat clinging to it. Her face glowed with pleasure. I grimaced and took an exaggerated sniff.

"What happened?" she said to Charro.

He glanced at me. "Take that look off your face." Then he muttered something to her from the far corner of his mouth.

I wiped my forehead. "What did you say?"

He shook his head.

"What did you *say*?"

"I was talking to Mirna, not to you."

"Don't talk in front of me like that."

He kissed his teeth. "I said, *this* is what I have to put up with."

I went into the salón but there were too many drunk people shouting, and speaking Spanish exhausted me, so I stood by myself, watching. Jorge's woman arrived, splendid and dark in a red dress that clung to her voluptuous frame. Her hair was set and curled, like a starlet from another time.

I lay down on Ramón's lumpy bed, and shivering in the chill wind of dusk covered myself with a ragged candlewick bedspread. I rolled into a ball, hands in front of my face, but I could not shut out the fretful, insistent shouting of the guests. It seemed to be inches away, just outside the window and ringing from the walls.

I dozed off and was woken by a rustling sound near my head. A sandwich sat in greaseproof paper on the bedside table, next to a bottle of orange squash. Charro was just inside the door: "Are you hungry?"

I sat up. Maybe it could be like Havana again—the red book, the pound coin, his eyes not hard.

"Anna, are you hungry?"

"Think so."

I held my hand out. He came and sat on the bed and watched me eat; after a few bites I stopped.

"Más," he said. "Come más."

I finished the sandwich. He pulled a little packet of biscuits from his pocket and fed them to me one by one.

"I'm sorry… I didn't mean… before—"

"—Anna, drop it. It's over."

"I didn't understand. Why are you so impatient?"

"You are fuerte. Sometimes."

"I have to be. I have to make sure—"

"—you don't have to understand everything, Anna." He scrunched the greasy sandwich paper up into his fist.

Later, I got up to take photographs against the chipped white walls, where spectral shadows were cast by the neon strip above. Each couple took a turn, posing formally, but when I went to snap them dancing, Ramón, inexplicably, said No.

Charro was propped in the window frame, a beer in his hand. My watch said half past one.

"Can we go back now please?" I said.

He didn't look at me.

"Back to Havana?" I touched his arm.

"I'm staying." His eyes were filmy, he was a bit drunk.

"Please. I want to go back to Lidia's. I'm so tired."

"Here in Cuba, when you go to a party it's for all the night—"

"—but I need to rest."

"I sleep in the street if I have to." He shrugged.

The music was distorted and the guests were bumping into each other like dodgems.

"OK." I took his hand but it felt dead. "Let's stay then."

The bass was all there was of the music, a rattle from too-loud speakers. My skull throbbed.

"What are you thinking?" he said.

"Nothing." I knew if I started talking it would go all wrong.

"What are you thinking?" His hand shook as he brought the beer to his mouth.

I didn't reply.

Ramón came over. He touched Charro's arm. "Is she enjoying the party?"

"We're leaving." Charro said.

Ramón looked pained. "What do you want to go back to Havana for?"

Charro nodded in my direction. Ramón looked at me and walked off.

I turned to Charro. "Stop speaking about me like that!

You're always angry—it's not fair. I've been trying to understand and speak Spanish for hours. I'm tired and I haven't done anything wrong."

He got up and pushed through the guests to the bedroom. I followed but didn't go in.

"... taxi ... hasta La Habana ... " Charro was saying. *A taxi to Havana*. It was all I could make out over the din. Just past the curtain that served as a door I could see Mirna cradling Frankie on the bed, and Ramón, who was pacing up and down.

I pushed back the curtain. "We're staying."

Ramón's little eyes were inscrutable behind his glasses. I didn't think it was anything deep—just the rum. He slung an arm round Charro and pulled him back to the party room.

"Charro has had too much to drink." I addressed Mirna on the bed.

"He says our place isn't comfortable enough for you or as nice as your room in Havana." There was no warmth in her eyes.

"It's not true! I don't think that—"

She got up and brushed past me, leaving Frankie rolling on the bed.

I shut myself in a little room with a broken propeller slung next to a child's wooden bed and brown medicine bottles, their contents long since evaporated.

Later, Charro came.

"I didn't say that to Mirna." Tears splashed down his face. I had never seen him cry before. I kneeled on the bed and threw my arms around him, smoothing his hair.

"Why are you crying?"

"Ramón was crying before. He is my family and I feel it too… The guests did not want to stay—the old woman wanted to leave so they all had to go. Ramón bought the meat. He made special things for them and they did not want to stay."

"Ramón's a grown man! Why would he cry over that?"

"We're in Cuba and we feel things."

I turned his face to mine. "But you hate it when I cry. You told me I should only do it when somebody dies."

We lay down head to toe in the little wooden bed. The sheet's childish patterns cradled a broken sleep.

I woke up at 3am to find him putting on his shoes and saying, "We're going, we're leaving, going back to Havana." He sat for a while, then fell back down into a stupefied sleep.

I stared into the black silence above the bed. Fragments of conversation rang inside my head, a mixture of English and Spanish. *Somos demasiado diferentes*, I heard myself say. *We are too different*. That is what I would tell him when we were gone from here, as if we had never been. I saw them — Charro, Ramón, Mirna and Frankie — getting smaller and smaller, further and further away, like the last white point in a dying TV.

I opened my eyes to the morning light. It was hot, with wind in many trees. There were voices and a never-ending stream of water, like being out at sea.

Charro lay next to me, recovering from the drink. I stroked my fingers over the dark shadows under his eyes, his desiccated lips.

He went to heat water for me to wash. I peered through the shutters at the street below, where lemons and red, pebbly mangoes hung heavy from the trees, and fraying palms blistered in the sun.

"Here." He handed me a bucket of hot water and I sat in the blue bathroom cascading it down my body until I was clean.

Last night seemed madness and I couldn't tell if it was Cuba or Charro.

The little table in the crook of the corridor had been set for two. Mirna served us coffee with salt and powdered milk, which I forced down so as not to appear rude. I had the guest cup, while Charro drank out of a glass. We ate white bread and butter. Charro put three spoons of sugar into his salty coffee.

A heavily pregnant woman arrived and I stared at her. It wasn't that I stared but I looked for much longer than I would have done at home, as if time had stretched.

Noon. I was slumped in the sofa, trapped and frustrated like an animal, thinking: *I am never coming here again*. Charro just kept saying "we'll go", and five minutes later "we'll stay for lunch". But I wasn't hungry. I didn't want to eat anything else. I wanted to go.

The dog was licking a bone in a tin can. The dog had a name but Charro didn't know what it was. The dog was white, with a nicotine-yellow tinge to its coat; it held down the bone with one paw, grating for every last scrap of meat.

Charro and Ramón were already drinking rum with limes.

"Honey, where is the Los Van Van CD? Did you bring it?" Charro was rifling through my rucksack.

"Here." I pulled it out.

He leaned an elbow on my shoulder, and scythed it across to Ramón. We set up my CD Walkman in the corner of the room; the ghetto blaster from last night had disappeared. My travel speakers sent out a tinny sound and the electricity kept cutting out.

"Dance with me. I need my inglesa." Charro pulled me up. At first, I looked past him and could barely move. My limbs were stiff. Then something began to flow through them, like oil from his, and we circled the floor. Ramón grinned from him to me, a shaft of sun glancing off his glasses. Charro kissed my neck and then my mouth.

When you were inside all the time the room seemed bright.

Mirna sat in the red plastic rocking chair feeding Frankie. She got up and reached into the fridge, where there were hundreds of little brown bottles, packets and pills. Then I remembered: she was a doctor. She took out a bottle, Frankie propped on one hip, and poured pinkish medicine into his mouth. Her silence was making me nervous. I cracked a few jokes and they all laughed; I couldn't tell if it was just polite. Then they referred to "when Charro comes to England" but I kept my gaze on the CD Walkman, which I was trying to get started again. I held the silver disc in my hands and imagined it on the shelf in the room in Havana. I saw the pile of writing paper by my bed and the unfinished letter to my mother, the fountain pen she had given me just before I left—"because if there's no email and no phone, you'll have to do the old-fashioned thing and write".

LEAVING CUBA

I AM WOKEN by Suci, the village postman, knocking at our door.

"Pavel," he calls, coming round to tap the shutters of my room. "I've got a letter for you—from Havana!"

It's not often that we get letters at my house—just once or twice a year. I jump out of bed and pull on my trousers, hitting my foot against the chair in my excitement. This will be the letter I have been awaiting for almost two months now—everyone in the village knows.

Suci is fanning himself with a papaya leaf that has fallen onto the porch. His face gleams with sweat but his blue post office shirt is neatly pressed, as if he's just put it on. In one hand he holds a white envelope, which bears a black embossed crest.

"Well, Pavel," he says. "I think you've got your answer right here."

I tear open the envelope and pull out the letter. Suci leans against the doorpost and watches me read.

"L'Ambassade de la République Française, La Havane, Cuba" it says. This is printed in large black letters at the top

of the page, then underneath, in Spanish, it says: "Dear Mr
Martinez, I am pleased to advise you that your application
for a French tourist visa has been successful. You will find
enclosed your passport, endorsed with a visa valid for six
months from the date of your proposed entry to France. I
would remind you of your signed statement that you will
undertake no employment during your stay, and that you
will not marry whilst in the French Republic. Please accept
my best wishes for a pleasant trip. Yours etc. Mme Fournet
on behalf of M. Beaulieu, French Ambassador to Cuba."

I tremble slightly as I read and it takes me some time. For
a good minute after I have finished I do not raise my eyes
because I am struggling to stop a tear from running down my
cheek. When I regain my composure, I look at Suci, whom
I have known since primary school, and a wide grin breaks
across my face.

"Congratulations my friend," he says.

Inside the house, my grandmother, Soledad, is standing by
the kitchen door. She is looking at me with an expression I
have never seen on her face before—there is defeat in her
eyes. But as I get closer, she pulls herself up. "What were
you thinking, Pavel, leaving the pigs thirsty for so long?
Go—fetch some water from the tank and let them drink.
Then, please, buy me two pounds of rice from the village
store." Even though it's nearly 11 o'clock, her kerchief is still
tied around her head, which means she's not yet combed her
hair, and she seems nervous, wiping her hands repeatedly
on her apron.

I do not think of Soledad for long, though. There are only
seven days to go before I take the aeroplane from Havana
to Paris, and much to do. I hurry to fetch water for the pigs.

I am a baker by trade, but the village bakery closed some
time ago because of flour shortages, so I work as a porter at
the tourist hotel. I won't pretend it's interesting, but I like to

watch the ocean, and the compañeros are pleasant enough.

The hotel is where I met Marianne. She came, like many others, for a holiday—but unlike the others, Marianne came back. We've been novios for nearly a year now, and she says it's time I visited her home. If you'd told me before I met her that I'd see another country one day, I would have laughed. I think I'd have been forever content to sit beside the ocean, watching the waves and fishing, or playing dominoes in the shade.

Tito is still snoozing on the sofa as I pull on my boots and leave for the village store. Sun through the shutter lights his dark brown cheek. He is at college in M—, the nearest town, but as it's summer, they are on holiday. Tito is my cousin, but I have lived with him, my aunty Lali and Soledad ever since my parents died. Last night, which belongs now to another time, we sat, Tito and I, on the porch and watched the stars. I asked him if they would look the same from Paris, but he said he did not know.

I make my way up the dirt track to the main road, and the village store.

Our neighbour is out on the porch with her husband. "Buen viaje!" she shouts with a wink—it seems Suci has delivered the news. Under the eaves of the neighbours' house, which leans precariously towards the bedroom that I share with Soledad, their son Adelmo is skinning a pig. I helped them kill it yesterday—Adelmo felt too much pity to draw the knife. He will do the same for me when it's time to slaughter our herd.

When I return home with the rice, Soledad is nowhere to be seen. The house is neat and tidy, today's washing on the line, and Tito is awake. He grins at me from his seat in the yard. The sun is high now; he squints through the light, a cafecito in one hand.

"Hermano," he says. "So—your journey begins."

I sit down next to him. We watch the hens as they pluck grain from the dirt.

"The peppers have done well since we planted them last month," I say.

"They have." Tito looks into his cup, which is empty now. "When are you going to tell Neta about your trip?" Tito is ten years younger and shouldn't tell me what to do. He doesn't catch my eye but gazes out at the glossy green banana forest in the yard. "Neta must not be the last to know."

"Leave that to me," I say. A hen squawks and jumps into the guava tree. "How could I forget Neta? She's my sister—all I have."

I say goodbye to Tito and go to the road to hitch a lift to Neta's village, S—. One or two people are waiting there already. We nod, say nothing and wait. Sometimes the trucks come, sometimes they don't. The road is dusty and very quiet, the little bar is closed. I swat a fly from my forehead and stare up into the sky.

Three hours later, I ride into S— on the back of a logging truck. Osbél, my brother-in-law, is waiting in his trap by the side of the road.

"Tito called the post office," he says. "Told them you were coming—let's go."

His horse whinnies and scratches at the ground. I jump in and we drive off, waving to friends along the street. It seems everyone knows I'm going away—everyone but Neta, that is: the farm is outside S— and doesn't have a phone.

"My friend, you've drawn the trump card, have you not?" Osbél's blue eyes glitter. "What will you do out there with your woman? Make a fortune and bring her back?"

I don't know exactly what I'll do in France but I've formed a kind of picture, so I hazard a guess. "I'll be working," I say. "Any kind of thing—repay Marianne the money she's spent."

"Plenty of work out there for the likes of you, I should think." Osbél whips the horse. "A strong fellow, not afraid of hard labour. What do they do in Paris to earn a crust? Not till the soil, that's for sure." He whips the horse again. "A few months of luxury and you won't want to come back home. No rations—all the food you can eat, I hear. And you earn what you need by working, no rules on what you keep."

"You don't know me, hermano, if you think I'll be tempted by those things." I look straight ahead at the road.

Osbél is silent.

"I, Pavel, will be coming back. Ours is the only free country in the world—*Cuba libre*—nothing can compare."

In truth, I am filled with curiosity for this new place but these are thoughts I can no longer share. It's not like talking with Osbél about the birds we'll catch when we hunt, or when he teases me, predicting that I'll shoot fewer than he does. Nor is it like when we imagine my future wife and child, living in a house as sweet as his, which he'll help me build. I have entered a place where I must walk alone.

We draw up to the farm. Neta is in front of the house, treading about in the manure. There's a shout and scuffling behind us as we get down from the trap; Tomás, Neta's son, rushes up with a little friend. They stop short when they see me with Osbél, and Tomás runs to Neta, hiding behind her legs.

"Brother." Neta kisses my cheek. She pulls Tomás forward. "Say hello to your uncle. Come on, don't be rude." He steps towards me, staring with his mother's eyes, which are also mine, and reaches up for a kiss. Then he darts off to play.

"They're setting snares for the rabbits," she says. "I've told them it's no good with all the dogs round here but they want to catch us dinner—*so Papi can take a rest*." She smiles with her mouth but not her eyes and brushes at her overalls, which are splashed with mud. "Come, brother, sit with us and talk."

The whiteboard house that Osbél has built is so new I can still smell damp in the palm leaves that make up the roof. Neta serves us cold coconut milk and slices of bread with margarine. When she's done, she pulls up a chair next to her husband and looks at me hard — she knows that something's up. Osbél is scraping at his plate to get the last crumbs into his mouth and for a while no one says a thing.

"It's some time since breakfast," Osbél says at last.

"He's up every dawn to work on the tobacco." Neta rubs a hand over her eyes. "It's more than one man's work, but the committee's sent everyone else to cut the cane."

Osbél is looking at me — I have to tell her.

"Neta…" I begin, but don't know how to put it. I start again. "Suci came this morning, with some news — I'm going to see Marianne."

Neta looks up from her cup. "What, Marianne's back in Havana?"

"No, Neta. It's not that."

She pulls her overalls around her as if it's cold. "You're going away?" Neta has never believed my trip will happen. "Finally, the visa came through?" Her eyes do not move from a point slightly to the left of my face, where they have come to rest. They are slow and very large. She looks like Tomás, about eight years old.

I reach for her hand. "It's not what you think, it's not for good."

Neta gets up to clear the table. "What happy news for Marianne." Her voice is faint and plates rattle against the sink as she puts them down. Then she wheels around and looks me in the eye. "What about Lucia's husband? Twenty years of a three-week husband once a year — from what I hear he made those promises to his family when *he* left. Who knows whether he's got a mistress in *Florida* — whatever it is that keeps him there, there's plenty of money to buy poor Lucia gadgets, televisions and the like, toys for the grandchildren from their once-a-year grandpa. And don't forget, they won't let you back for a long while after you leave—"

"—Neta, that's enough." Osbél lifts a harness from the wall and strides outside.

I look at the flagstones because I can't bear to see my sister cry. "Neta, listen. Thirty-two years I've lived content with what I have. They could pile beef onto my plate, fill my wallet with dollars—it wouldn't change a thing."

Neta stands at the sink, head pressed into her palms. I put my arm around her shoulders.

She turns to look up at me, quiet now. "I hope to God you're right."

It is night; the family is asleep. My bonita Marianne looks out from the photograph I hold in my hand.

When she last came to visit, she showed me pictures of her apartment. "Right in the centre of Paris," she said. "Near all my friends, everything—we'll have such a good time."

She promised to show me many things: shops that sold all you could want under one roof—shoes and food and clothes, towers that stretched up to the sky, trains that travelled beneath the sea.

The floors of her apartment were covered in carpet; paper with roses adorned the wall. In my house the floors are stone, and there are no flowers—just yellow paint.

"Are you afraid of going on the plane?" she asked.

Now, in the darkness, her words echo in my room.

"Of course not, Marianne," I said.

It wasn't quite the truth. I have never been on a plane before—when I thought of flying up there among the stars I felt a little scared, but she would never know.

She was reassured and rested her head on my shoulder. "You look after me, Pavel... Like no one ever has."

My arm wrapped tighter round her. "Wherever we go, nena, at least I can do that."

Tonight, the memory of her voice fills my ears; I can still smell her skin. As the first strands of dawn creep over the mountains, I finally get some sleep.

The cockerel crows and I open my eyes. I am in my bed. It's my last day in the village; tomorrow I leave for Havana.

Neta arrives with Tomás, and the family gathers in the front room to help me pack. All that I will need fits into the blue sports bag I take to the beach: my best black trousers and shirt, khakis—good for every day, underwear, vest and two pairs of socks. My shoes, of course, will be on my feet.

Lali says: "Aren't you going to pack your jeans?"

I frown, and answer more grumpily than I mean to: "You don't wear jeans in the city—they're for hunting with Osbél."

Lali looks at Soledad and rolls her eyes.

"Do as Lali tells you," my grandmother says.

I go to the closet and pull them out. "Well, I suppose they might be good for work."

Neta is silent. She's holding Tomás to her and he's straining to break free. Standing, he fits under her arm; his bright brown eyes watch my every move. Then he pulls away and runs outside. Neta watches him go.

"Be careful of the cold," she says to me.

"Yes, be careful—their weather's not like ours." Soledad looks worried. "Here, take these" —she hands me three flat packages wrapped in greaseproof paper— "so you won't go hungry on the plane." It's touron: she spent all yesterday afternoon grinding sesame seeds to make me this.

"And don't go out on the streets," adds Neta. "The people

are violent, it's very dangerous—you might get picked on by a criminal if you go outside."

Lali's quiet, but then she pipes up: "If you get lonely come back straight away. I've heard the people there are very mean—take your money but won't be your friend—old people sleeping on the streets."

"Of course I won't be lonely." I zip the bag shut. "It's not difficult—you want friends, just be friendly. If I find myself alone, I'll stop an agreeable looking fellow and explain I'm new in town."

One part of me believes this, another is not so sure. The films we get from abroad show things that never happen here; foreigners seem to solve all their problems using guns, and while I know how to use a gun, it's not the kind the movies show.

Early the next morning, before the sun is up, I walk to the cemetery to say goodbye to my parents. The dawn crickets are chirping as I go to the grave. When I return, Neta, Soledad, Tito and Lali are waiting on the porch. Soledad presses a five-dollar bill into my hand.

"Take it," she says. "Something to help you on your way." A single tear is lodged in the corner of her eye.

With the bag slung over my shoulder I set off for the road. I can't look back. The last thing I hear is Tomás shouting: "Goodbye, uncle, goodbye! Don't forget, you promised to bring me a boat." When a water truck rolls past, I stop it and jump on. As we reach the edge of the village my house shrinks, with my family waving on the porch, bumping up and down in time to the wheels of the truck.

When we draw into Havana eight hours later, my cousin Frank is waiting in his Chevrolet to take me to the tower block where he lives. I have a shower and we walk over to his mother's house to eat.

Frank pulls a photograph from a drawer after dinner. "Her name was Annie. We met in a London bar."

Frank has been abroad—he worked on ships and stopped in ports around the world. The girl in the picture is grinning and has long red hair. Frank is by her side, slimmer than now, one arm around her waist.

"She was fun. The people there were kind." Frank puts the picture back into the drawer and shuts it. He looks sad. "Make the most of your chance, cousin—don't let opportunity pass you by."

Today is my last day in Cuba. I spend it helping Frank fix his car, which has suddenly refused to start. We're not talking much—the work's too hot—but if I wanted to, Frank would listen. We connect a temporary petrol tank to the engine with a rubber tube—it should be good for tonight's run to the airport and back.

Afterwards, we sit on the balcony, sixteen floors up, with a bottle of rum.

"Taking a final look?" Frank asks, as I lean over the rusty balustrade. My back is sweaty and there's engine oil under my nails but I want to stand here for a while before I wash. The city is orange now, sky a burning red, huge globe of sun sinking to the sea. It is strangely quiet. From up here the people look like ants, and the smells of decomposing rubbish are gone.

"Marianne will be waiting for you at the other end." Frank puts a hand on my shoulder. "Six months isn't long."

I say nothing. The longest I've been away from home is a week.

Frank half-smiles as he pours the rum; the slanting sun catches his spectacles.

"Salud," he says.

"Salud." I raise my glass.

Only Frank comes with me to the airport. I wanted it like this. Half-way there the car grumbles to a halt, but with some minor tinkering we get it started again. As we step into the departure hall I can still smell petrol on Frank's shirt. The only other Cubans there are guards.

A line of foreign tourists winds back towards the door. We join it. The sign at the front says *Air France*—this must be my plane.

The official behind the desk looks closely at my papers. Sweat pricks my armpits. She takes a full minute to check each page: visa, exit stamp, ID. But then she raises her head and smiles: "Your first time out?"

I nod.

"Well—enjoy the trip. Passport control is to your left and down the stairs."

In front of us is a line of booths. You step inside and shut the door. If they let you through, a buzzer sounds, the light goes green, and you push open a door to the other side.

The official in my booth looks at me for a long time; I look back. He rustles my documents and sighs, then picks up a stamp and brings it down on my passport, which he pushes back to me under the glass.

The buzzer is so loud that it shuts out everything else. I see Frank mouthing, *goodbye*. In front of me is the door, behind me Frank. I pause for seconds, minutes almost, looking back. The official taps on the glass and the buzzer sounds again.

Frank's face is frozen. I am looking at his face and he is smiling, but the smile is very small. It is printed onto my mind as I reach the other side because the lights there are so bright I have to stop for a minute and close my eyes. When I open them I see a bank of shops. Neon flashes off diamond and steel, sickly perfume fills the air. I cannot breathe.

I make for some benches where people are sitting, and take a plastic bottle filled with orange drink from my bag. I sip on it to settle my stomach. Crushed into a corner at the bottom of the bag I find the touron that Soledad made; the greaseproof paper has torn and it's gathered bits of fluff.

People start to move. I follow them towards the gate.

Inside, the plane is like the bowel of an enormous boat—so many seats I cannot see the end. Everyone else is already sitting; I look at the number on my ticket and find my place.

As we take off, there is a roar and my body glues heavy to the seat. I close my eyes and see only darkness. When I open them again, a map of stars hangs beneath me—then I realise the stars are city lights.

Nothing has been this beautiful before: Havana, like magic, all in one.

BREATHE

I saw him for the first time under the night and he didn't smile. It was in his eyes, though. When I told him where I came from, he seemed to understand.

I came from a place where they stole your life, a place that forgot all time in its haste. Every day there was less air, till the people would lie gasping in the streets, crushed together, fighting to stay alive. This was the place where I lived.

"Meet Serafín," said Luis. "He is the man who brings you your air. He fills the tanks for when you dive."

He sloped between me, back and forth; I stood and watched him as he went.

Each day, at the same time, he had a bucket of water and walked the length of the beach beside the huts, long low and sloping.

When Luis told him: "Come, Serafín, come and meet the girls," he took my hand and did not smile.

I was here, I was waiting and I didn't much care, so long as I could forget. I'd smoke a cigarette by the ocean, take my dives with the rest, reaching tranquil oblivion at the bottom of the sea.

After the dives I sat in the bar with the other tourists, slept early, or stayed awake counting the stars with the freezing breeze inside my room. You could wrap yourself in a blanket there, while the workers sat outside playing cards, beating off the flies and sweat.

His face was flat planes, sharp sun reflected off the sides. He didn't quite look at me, though somehow he knew.

In the bar, the Cubans were playing dominoes. Serafín was there; he held in his hand a glass of white rum. As I walked past, thinking to sit alone and read, I was stopped. A hand reached out—in it, a glass of rum.

Smiles dared him in the hush.

"Drink?" He held out the glass with a tiny grin at the side of his mouth. I took it, daring to look back.

Relief all round. They returned to the game, to the black clicking counters and the tiny white spots.

All I could see from my stool at the bar was the curly black back of Serafín's head.

Morning. A mosquito came to bite my pale skin, naked on the sheet. Beyond the window, shutters opened to blue dawn and the life outside.

The faun swirls of the curtain looked as if they had been painted with a brush onto its peachy lace. Behind them, a spray of green-and-gold leaves held off the morning sun. I was cool, turned in white blankets—iced air humming in to kill the blaze.

I took a walk, a long walk. It seemed to me that everything was sitting, just sitting there, phasing in and out of sleep. The air was sweet and slow. An invisible thread, a meniscus, surrounded the place.

I saw a fan pattern everywhere—a fan pattern in the palms, in the coral, running along the lines of the shore underneath the sea.

But though the air was clean here, I couldn't find a way to breathe. At night, we'd lie about on the warm sand, all of us divers from the group, blowing plumes of our smoke into the curious glow of the dark. We'd watch how they weaved, and marvel at what we saw without the glare of city lights.

We drank, and sought our solace in each other—in crisp dry couplings that took place after careful lurching journeys to our separate rooms.

A week went by like this, and then we had to go.

I walked along the scrub path beyond the beach. Serafín was standing at the back of the boiler room filling up the tanks.

"I've come to say goodbye," I told him. "We're leaving here today."

He drew me forward to kiss my cheek.

"Quédese, un día más."

I wrinkled up my brow, and he thought for a minute until he found the words: "Stay... one more day."

So the others went on without me.

I came in the night and he was there in a clean pressed shirt, leaning into his chair, nonchalant.

I waited. Sat at the bar. I waited, sat alone.

His eyes, when he pulled up a stool in one sudden move, his eyes enclosed me and we talked.

"Buenas noches," he said.

"Serafín."

"You are well?"

"A little tired."

"And the diving? Good today?"

"As usual."

He brushed the fingers of one hand over the surface of the bar. "And you? Happy to go home?"

"… No …"

He nodded, waiting to hear more.

"My city, it is very big: *grande*," —I held my arms wide— "a million people. A jungle."

"Ah sí, un millón." He looked at me, listening without surprise.

It was a little late, a little time had passed, and we were dancing. One by one the other people left. There were just three tourists sitting at a table by the door, mulling over a last glass of beer.

In the middle of the dance floor, he took my hand in his. He rocked in front of me: slow, simple, moving from side to side.

My glass was on a table and I knocked it to the floor. He went behind the bar to get another. The tourists came over and asked me to join them for a nightcap in their room but I did not go.

Then it was just us.

"Are you tired?" he said

"Yes." I was sitting. "Are you?"

"No. Not me—come." He took my hand and led me up from the chair, under the big palms to the shore, and lay me onto the sand.

His eyes were black; mine, hard bore in.

The seashore sloped up quick. The small waves lapped away in the silence of other people's sleep; just us — no noise could wake them.

He bit my flesh. I didn't mind. Smelled the blood like it was mine and his reached together. A cry, it was mine, from my mouth — and dog-fast breath in his.

And then the silence. Side by side, minutes from the shore we were wrapped. But the light would come.

"I will go," he said.

"With me — to my room."

"No." The last moon shone behind him. "No. Not possible. I to my room, you to yours." He drew me to my feet.

"What will you do? Tomorrow, will you know me Serafín?"

He didn't flinch: "I know you."

And then he turned to go — to escape the light, which had slid one grey finger above the line of the sea.

I lay awake with pictures of the night. They hovered clean and clear; I held them there like bells.

Day. I sat on the step outside my room, watching the water in the early morning sun. Serafín came from his hut along the path.

He nodded me to come — didn't give his hand.

Past scrubbed brush till the path petered out, along the sea I followed, catching him up as the beach became end over a low concrete wall. Beyond was thick green; the shore was even and tight, fishes beneath the water.

"Look — barracuda," he said.

A mammoth ugly fish with teeth trawled low by my feet.

We crossed a wire; he helped me under, I followed on. There were green palms dense to one side and a terrific bird-noise ringing out. Red petals speckled the path we walked.

We came to the side of a shallow pool; he sat and I next to him, staring into the emerald green.

Lace again, on the seabed, and little brown fishes, dithering in the pools. Sea so warm we spent hours basking in the waves, watching as the light drained to crimson from a sun-stripped sky. White in your eye like a day-long flash and heat that wrapped you in an airless cloak, sweating from each fold of the skin.

Serafín swam far out and sat alone on a jutting crag.

A closed circle between sea and sky and bush, sealed to form the perfect space.

He stood, then arched into a dive. White surfing tongues lapped the sapphire sea as he reached the shore and sat, legs pulled up beneath, examining the shell of a dead crab. His feet were square, each polished toe scrubbed and dusted by the sand.

"Give me your hand," he said.

I gave it.

"Now—breathe."

Grass waved backwards on its haunches in the end of the day, shoals of purple and yellow fish rushed around the coral, and I closed my eyes as the last ray of sun crossed the water to land on the sand.

GLOSSARY

amore my love
amorosa loving
ay, mi madre sweet mother of God
baila dance
el baño the bathroom
bonita pretty
caliente hot
cara dear
carajo fuck
chancletas flip-flops
chiquitica very little (of a girl)
claro of course
come más eat more
cómo anda? how's it going?
compañero comrade
con calma calmly
coño dammit
cuántos años? how old?
cubana Cuban woman
dale, compañeros come on, comrades
dame un beso give me a kiss
déjame leave me alone
dime tell me
Dios mío my God
doble moral double standard
ella entiende she understands
estás linda como el mamey you are as beautiful as the mamey
este carro de mierda this shitty car
extranjeros foreigners
frijoles beans
fuerte forceful
guapa good-looking
hermano brother (a friendly greeting, not always literal)

inglesa English woman
jinetera literally 'jockey'; a Cuban woman who dates a foreign man with financial benefit in mind
el líder the leader
locas crazy women
luchando struggling on
maldito damned
mamita sweetheart
más more
más gordita fatter
me da pena contigo I've let you down
me encanta Cuba I love Cuba
mierda shit
mi hijita my little daughter
mira cómo le da pena look how embarrassed she is
mira cómo le gusta mover el culo look how she likes to move her arse
mira, hermano look, brother
muchas nalgas big buttocks
mucho gusto a pleasure to meet you
muy intenso very intense
negocio business
nena sweetie
no lo quiero así I don't want it like that
novio boyfriend
pasta con carne y jugo de mango pasta with meat and mango juice
por interés for ulterior motives
por la calle on the street
precioso sweet
puttana bitch
qué bolá? how's it going?
qué linda how pretty

qué pena what a pity
qué quieres? what do you want?
quinceañera party to celebrate a girl's 15th birthday
salud cheers
sei bellissima you are very beautiful
siempre luchando always struggling
sin vergüenza without shame
soy cubano I'm Cuban
te oí hablando ingles I heard you speaking English
tésis thesis
una relación decente a respectable relationship
ven come in
venga come on
vete. ahora, ve a tu mamá go. go to your mother now
vete, cámbiate go, get changed
la vieja the old lady
viejo old man
yo la creé I formed her

Lightning Source UK Ltd.
Milton Keynes UK
UKOW03f2335300317
297926UK00001B/1/P

9 780954 157050